CW00434642

THE LOVER AND INTERPRETER OF HUMAN ODDITIES

A NOVELLA

ANTHONY LABRIOLA

ANAPHORA LITERARY PRESS

QUANAH, TEXAS

ANAPHORA LITERARY PRESS
1108 W 3rd Street
Quanah, TX 79252
https://anaphoraliterary.com

Book design by Anna Faktorovich, Ph.D.

Printed in the United States of America, United Kingdom and in Australia on acid-free paper.

Cover Image: "Zimní elegie" (2009) painting by Eugene Ivanov.

Published in 2019 by Anaphora Literary Press

The Lover and Interpreter of Human Oddities: A Novella
Anthony Labriola—1st edition.

Library of Congress Control Number: 2018966168

Library Cataloging Information

Labriola, Anthony, 1950-, author.
    The lover and interpreter of human oddities: A novella / Anthony Labriola
    74 p. ; 9 in.
    ISBN 978-1-68114-490-0 (softcover : alk. paper)
    ISBN 978-1-68114-491-7 (hardcover : alk. paper)
    ISBN 978-1-68114-492-4 (e-book)
1. Fiction—Psychological. 2. Fiction—Suspense.
3. Fiction—Literary.
PN3311-3503: Literature: Prose fiction
813: American fiction in English

DEDICATION

To all the lovers and interpreters of life's stories, especially my own storytelling family—Louisa Josephine, Anthony, Michelle, Simon, Nic, Samantha, Lucy, Christina and Joanna

"The laborious process of causation which sooner or later will bring about every possible effect, including (consequently) those which one had believed to be most nearly impossible, naturally slow at times, is rendered slower by our impatience (which in seeking to accelerate only obstructs it) and by our very existence, and comes to fruition only when we have ceased to desire it—have ceased, possibly, to live."
—From *Within a Budding Grove* in *Remembrances of Things Past* (Volume 1)
by Marcel Proust (translated by C.K. Scott Moncrieff)

PART ONE

The Group Fiction[1]

1
THE DETECTIVE

"I will start out this evening with an assertion: fantasy is a place where it rains."
—From *Six Memos for the Next Millennium* by Italo Calvino (translated by Patrick Creagh)

'm ready to unpack my testimony. It hangs on certain events that occurred at that odd and remarkable time of my life. I take full responsibility for what happened then, the consequence of which put a violent end to my *Truth Parties*.

As Dr. Clive Wango, real estate tycoon and self-styled healer, I owned a multi-million dollar mansion in the upscale and secluded neighbourhood of the city's north end. The Don River Valley and lush parklands surrounded my high-walled compound. Since I believed in the curative power of life stories, I spared no expense for clients in conflict, and, for the sake of group therapy, paid the price in more ways than one. With no disrespect intended to victims of systemic injustice, I sought truth and reconciliation. Where truth and fiction were concerned, I took a no-holds-barred attitude for the simple reason that I wanted to protect my *people* from further violence and <u>disillusionment</u>. To that end, I offered them the *talking* cure. But as

1   From *Dragonfly's Urban Crusade* (Anaphora Literary Press, 2017)

host of the Truth Parties, I found that the more we talked, the closer we got to the *love* cure. Of course, love doesn't always come cheap or easy.

One of the two *guests* still at the palatial mansion from the previous night's group fiction was a young, pesky detective. I knew he had a truth-obsession, but I'd soon discover that he specialized in threats of the *fantastical*. Was it all high fantasy? Was it just imagination? And what was *that*?

"Imagination is a place where it rains *inside*,[2]" the Detective said.

He wore a black, feathered helmet, a short, black cape, a black, hooded sweatshirt, with a black t-shirt under it, and tapered, tightfitting, black jeans, as well as two-toned black and white sneakers, but no socks. The fact that he had been implicated in the emotional massacre of opposing factions in last night's Truth Party now threatened to taint the next night's party with the allure of dark fantasy. After first leaving and then doubling back to pick up the weapons he'd left behind, the Detective claimed he could hear a shrill cry for help coming from somewhere in the rainy dark.

"Is it, in the aftermath of what went down last night, an auditory hallucination?" I asked.

"Maybe," he whispered, wheezing, as if to shush me, "but still you've got to have a good ear to hear what's going on in an hallucinatory night, especially like the one just past."

To improve his hearing, he flipped back the big, black hood of his cowl-neck hoodie. Then, dragonfly-like, just hovered there. As if in mid-air, the Detective considered all six directions, before propelling himself upward, downward, forward, backward, left or right.

"Might it be the dark fantasy of a stormy night, especially after what you've been through?" I suggested, needling him.

"Might be," he said, "could be, for those of you who like to link fantasy to dark and rainy nights."

"Did you hear cries for help in the surging sound of wind and rain?" I asked, on the point of suggesting a fugue state.

"I did," he gasped, "unless you or your partner are trying to distract me."

He was referring to my business partner, Zeus (Zoo) Majesky. He was the other guest still at the mansion from the previous party.

"Distracting *you* with a cry beyond *my* hearing?" I asked the Detective, because I just had to know.

2   See Dante Alighieri's *Purgatory* from *The Divine Comedy*.

"With shrieks and wails of terror," the Detective said, "that only *my* pricked-up ears can hear."

"Then maybe it's raining inside the mansion, so to speak," I said, trying to be witty to mask my fear, "and you should stay on and look into it."

"Can't just now," he said, "despite the allure of high fantasy. As you know, I'm on my honeymoon. But don't be frightened, Dr. Wango. Call me if you're in distress, and if it keeps raining down on you, and if I can come, I will. Later. Peace. Out."

He slung his black rucksack onto his bony back, humped his narrow shoulders, and then slamming down his long, lean, sleek skateboard to the wet ground, he pushed off. I had him under surveillance. The security camera tracked his every insect-like move. He looked like an insect: a dragonfly in black armour, say, just darting here and there. Now, doing skateboard tricks, and at last making his choice of directions, he left the mansion.

The Detective had helped to solve the case of a group of anarchists, hell-bent on destroying *Majesky and Wango Enterprises*. In doing so, he had also fallen in love with Zoo's secretary, a strikingly beautiful young woman named Miranda. After overcoming the *monster*, Zoo's ex, Hera (alias Mom), the couple had rushed up the designated staircase to the rooftop where a dragonfly-shaped helicopter waited for them there; and, after a lingering wave in farewell, and after a breathtaking kiss that had seemed to fuse them as one, they flew off together. And so, since it was time for going, they lifted off high above my upscale neighbourhood. Like a star-wheel, the helicopter's propeller had spun, riding in thin air, aiming for a vanishing point. The globe spinners were off on their whirlwind honeymoon. Teary-eyed, I could see from my observation tower, the helicopter, like a metallic insect, ascending until it appeared as a pinprick of light in the dark, tricky, night sky, now bursting and whirling with millions of stars.

"What's *he* doing back here?" Zoo asked, coming out of nowhere.

"Who, our hipster detective?" I asked.

"Who else am I talking about?"

"Well, our modern-day knight, dubbed Sir Dragonfly, is on another urban crusade."

"I thought he was with the love of his life, Miranda, on their honeymoon," Zoo said, riled, sidling up.

"He's honeymooning all right," I said. "But he forgot a few things from the last case and just popped by to retrieve his weapon of choice."

I downplayed how lethal the Detective's crossbow and arrows actually were.

"He really gets around on that skinny skateboard, eh?" Zoo sneered.

"If the terrain permits," I said. "But if it doesn't, he just straps on his rollerblades for comfort and speed, and then you should see him on the stairs."

"I've seen him on the stairs," Zoo said. "I went skateboarding with him once, remember?"

"I remember," I said. "I tried in vain to get him to stay for my new case, but he couldn't."

"Another carnival of human oddities, your next case?" Zoo demanded.

"You said it. I didn't."

"So, the Detective is on his *honeymoon* at last," Zoo said, "and sure as hell, he wouldn't stay. I know I wouldn't."

"I know *you* wouldn't," I said, "but he told me that if I need him, all I have to do is call him on his cell, honeymoon or no, and he'll come back in a flash."

"Weird," Zoo said. "He loves his work that much, does he?"

"He does," I said, "but, for the time being, he loves his Miranda just a little bit more."

It was the consciousness of all that, especially the cry, that had puzzled the Detective for a while. But, gifted in the art of sleuthing, and true to his art, he had said he would come back to discover the source. He would reveal it only when the time (or timing) was right. Good for you, true Detective… No wonder some poet wrote a ballad about you as an urban crusader,[3] and dubbed you Sir Dragonfly:

On his urban crusade, with lance-tipped thoughts
And see-through shield, this city knight, nicknamed Sir Dragonfly,
Is more than halfway there: East of Is and West of Seems,

Or North-Northwest, in the mad-brained mapping of his lost quest.
Like a hawk in direct line with the sun and the hunter's eye,
Sir Dragonfly mistakes the real route for the fabled way and
doubles back.

---

3   Based on the poem, "Dragon's Blood," from *Armour and Lace: From the Dragon Slayer's Notebook*, Anaphora Literary Press, 2017.

The faster he rides on his skateboard, the farther he has to go.
This quest-hero is an urban warrior with a hockey helmet on backwards,
And homemade crossbow in his black rucksack, wearing black
kneepads

And black elbow pads; like a dragonfly in black armour,
He hoists an avenging flag to break up a fight at the coffee shop.
He loads his quiver with Arrows of Longing.

So Sir Dragonfly weighs the pros and cons of dragon slaying, asking,
Are you in distress? Locked in a tower? Will you ever let down your hair?
Arrow-headed sunrays pierce his armour, now turning to lace.

And then he takes his place with space captains, hipster detectives,
Non-binary superheroes, urban knights, and civic vampire slayers,
And even sensitive werewolves.

Despite dark laughter, Sir Dragonfly strives to save us even from ourselves.
For it is still not a good day to die, but rather to live, and in living,
Live right, and still living, live on, and in living on, live on in
legend.

Zoo couldn't stand the ballad and started chafing me right away.

"No rest for you then, even after that horrible trouble with my Ex[4]?" he asked.

"Not for this wicked doctor," I said, "especially in my line of business."

"Real estate?"

"That, and the *Truth*."

So since there was no rest for me in my own quest, I decided to stay up for the remainder of the night. Zoo joined me in the night watch. I said something about *shoring up our thoughts against our ruins*. But he wouldn't have it, not if I were prepared to use poetry against him.

"By the way, with regard to these so-called truth parties of yours…"

"What about them?"

"Are they always in groups? Is there always a group *fiction*, to use

---

4   For information about that case, consult *Dragonfly's Urban Crusade*, Anaphora Literary Press, 2018.

your weird expression?"

"No, sometimes, party for two, or even one, depending on the stories they're telling themselves, stories that are self-blinding, for which the truth is the sole way out of their self-created darkness. If you stick around, you'll meet one of my *new* clients, a philosophy professor from the local university, complete with a group of academics dragging their hostilities behind them."

"What's his story?"

"From his letter and the dossier of his case, I'm given to understand that he *lost* his head, you see, or at least, he is telling himself that story, and claims he was *beheaded*. I'm interested in the symbolic truth of his story, and in giving him a chance to tell it his way, so he can deal with the conception or misconception of 'decapitation.'"

"Castration fantasy?"

"That's easy enough. Or maybe, a head-carrier, like those of old, but there is also a 'group fiction' or cluster of interlacing narratives involving the eyewitnesses and the 'constellation' of those involved in the case. The professor still senses a degree of lingering menace and spite towards him, and fears further provocation and torment. Are you interested? Are you staying?"

"I'll see," Zoo said. "If I'm interested, I'll stay once the *headless* man arrives, carrying his head in his hands."

I knew he didn't understand the case as I'd outlined it for him in my brief synopsis. Or he was just mocking the professor, and, at the same time, ridiculing me, as always. Zoo needed very little rest to go on, but he headed off to freshen up. If he stayed, I'd give him a champagne breakfast, and take care of my next guest (and his group) due to arrive early in the morning. I was eager to hear the story he was telling himself and others. I wanted him to sound the depth of his own truth and shatter his illusions with a little help from my wisdom and expertise. For him, the Absolute Centre of the Carpet (my usual staging ground for the session) was unnecessary. I had decided to take him out to the garden to get him to relate his tale. I'd also invited the others he spoke about in his letter to hear their versions of the "head" incident. This case also involved another psychotherapist, Dr. Luna Schlangenkopf, from the Wellness Centre North of Lake Superior. She was intimately acquainted with some of the "players" involved in the so-called beheading of Professor Karl Brainerd.

The group arrived at the mansion at nine that morning. Zoo was already out in the garden, sipping champagne and eating strawberries. He was smirking, wearing a plush, white housecoat, legs crossed, looking imperious. I introduced him to Professor Brainerd, a short, squat, bigheaded man in his sixties. He was at the centre of this case. I also introduced Zoo to two of the professor's students, Giuliana Koffmann, a tall, dark-haired and dark-eyed young woman, and Dylan Hedley, nicknamed *Odd*, a thin, bug-eyed young man. They were here as eyewitnesses. Then a couple of Brainerd's colleagues, Professor Athena Headborn, statuesque with short hair, and Professor Riddley Hodder, a crook-backed, bald man, and Professor Brainerd's attending physician, Dr. Bongo Scully, with his leading man good looks, whom I already knew, arrived and introduced themselves. There was also a man named Arjuna Sar, a fit-looking middle-aged man, apparently the porter at the University, who had just arrived on a Harley-Davidson.

The rain had given way to sunny weather. Breakfast was brought out to us at my next Truth Party. I seated my guests on white wicker chairs at outdoor tables. In the garden setting and under a glorious sun, I started with a few questions, and Professor Brainerd reluctantly told us his side of the *headless* truth.

2
STOLEN STORIES[5]

"She was at the age for which all stories are true and all conceptions
are stories."
—From *What Maisie Knew* by Henry James

"They are dragon-seekers, bent on improbable rescues."
—From "First Lesson" by Phyllis McGinley

Brainerd's account was strangely familiar to me, as if I'd heard
it (or read it) before. He told of an incident in philosophy
class when, goaded by Odd's questions, more of a cross-
examination about aesthetics than a typical philosophical quizzing
of Brainerd, the professor said that he had lost his head. Later that
morning, when Giuliana went to visit him in his office to discuss her
term paper and to accuse him of diminishing her as a *female* philosophy
student, Professor Brainerd smashed his head through the plate-glass
window. He then picked it up, dangling by the arteries, and headed off
to the hospital. Once there, he asked for (and received) treatment as
if it were merely a minor head injury, and not a medical miracle. Dr.
Bongo Scully had patched him up. Now, the academics in his circle
were obsessing about what this *head incident* really signified.[6]

My guests stayed out for a while and then I showed them to their
rooms. Zoo went for a naked dip in the pool and waited for me there.
This was his notion of a charm offensive.

"That was easy enough," he said, toweling off, giving me his opinion
of the case. "He's off his rocker, philosophy prof and all. He was likely
coming on to Giuliana. I know I would have. He was coming on to
her, and *lost* his head."

5   Passages, tales, and stories used here are originally to be found in
The Pros & Cons of Dragon-Slaying (Anaphora Literary Press).

6   The incident is recorded in the story, "The Severed Head."

"There's individual work to be done here," I said, ignoring his interpretation, "over the coming days, because of the hostility that exists in this collection of folks from the university."

"I can help you with Giuliana," Zoo said. "She's something else. So is the other one, Professor Athena."

"Thanks, but I think I'll just wait for back-up," I said, "and until I've met with them alone. Still, I like the idea of starting with Giuliana."

I invited her to take a little walk with me on the grounds. I showed her the pool, the fountain, the statuary. When we came to the archery range, she became agitated, but seemed intrigued, nonetheless. I asked her if she wished to do a bit of target practicing. She smiled. She then said she had some knowledge of archery, some skill, and was used to competition. But for the moment, she wasn't interested in shooting arrows. She expressed interest in the set-up and the equipment, its array and storage.

"Maybe later," she said, "I'll show you what I can do with a bow."

So, I escorted her into the garden—the labyrinth section. This would be an ideal setting for what I considered a life story with a maze at the centre of it. There were ways in, with only *one* way out. When I explained that to her, first she looked away and then directly at me.

"All right," she said. "The maze, yes, all right, Dr. Wango. Show me the way in, and I'll find the only way out by myself."

On the cusp of getting intimate and getting to know what her story was, Giuliana told me things about herself that included her odd view of *creating* her family. She also told me about her pet, a Jesus Lizard, that her father insisted was a *dragon*.

We entered the labyrinth and walked on. I was not leading the way.

"What are you after?" Giuliana asked me.

"Liberation from lies and reconciliation between opposing factions," I said.

Giuliana insisted that I was talking to her just like one of her psychotherapists, Dr. Luna Schlangenkopf, at the Mindfulness Centre North of Lake Superior.

"I spent some time in treatment there," she said, "as a result of my father's mental abuse."

She went on about her relationship with her father, and referred to him as a dragon slayer. She wanted to bring him down and cut him to pieces. I didn't want to get into castration fantasies. Well, I did, but not at this point in the labyrinth. She said her case was the subject of Dr.

Schlangenkopf's study of childhood terrors.

"I'm in her book," Giuliana said. "It's titled *Growing Backwards*. Have you read it?"

Before I could answer her that I was familiar with her therapist and her work, somebody was shouting at us from beyond the maze.

"Ignore him," she said, knowing *who* it was.

Giuliana was on the point of saying that her daddy's conception of her pet was a *Dragon of Desire*, but reconsidered and refused to do so. It was best not to talk about desire, she said, especially to me.

"What's that?"

"Someone is calling your name."

"It's Odd. He thinks he owns me, or believes he can rescue me, and can't ever have me out of his sight."

"Does he… own you, I mean?"

"He thinks so."

"You're out of sight now. Even if he tries to follow you, he can't find you."

"He'll find a way."

"Let him call out. No matter. I'll get to him soon."

"It's best not to talk about anything," Giuliana whispered. "He doesn't listen, anyway, and neither does anybody else."

I was scribbling furiously in my notepad: *She thinks men want to rescue her.*

"Go on," I said.

Our pace was so quick that we might appear to be running. Did she want out? What was she calculating? She was getting away from me, like a character in a story that will not do what the writer wants her to do. Would she have a panic attack? Was she sure she could find the exit by herself? She went on ahead of me, despite my warning.

"Can you hear me?" she shouted.

"I hear you," I said, but I didn't know if I were really listening to her or to the shouts on the outside of the maze. Odd, or whoever it was, was maniacally persistent.

"Can you hear me, now?" she asked.

"I hear you," I said.

"I'm nearly *there*," she said.

"So, this story or dream about your daddy is really about you," I shouted.

"Yes," Giuliana said, "I had to get out of there, just as I had to get out of this maze. I had to get away from my daddy, the dragon slayer, just as I have to get away from all of you."

3
READING THE GALLERY[7]:
ENDLESS STAIRS[8]

O nce we stepped out of the garden maze and headed back to the house, Odd was waiting for us. I didn't want to talk to him just then. But Giuliana had a thing or two to say to him and loudly spoke her piece.

"What are you yelling about?" Giuliana demanded.

"I didn't mean anything by it," he said. "Just wanted to see if you were safe."

"To control me, you mean," Giuliana said. "You're just weird. That's why I call you *Odd*."

She had words with him, then brushing past him, went inside. Maybe Odd and I could go for target practice on the archery range. I wanted to see if he'd let me in on what was going on. I was thinking jealousy, maybe resentment, certainly spite. Could it be passion? I told Odd I was going to freshen up and meet him later on the shooting range. If he didn't want to shoot arrows but guns, that could be arranged.

"Let's start with bows and arrows," I thought, "in memory of the Detective." He was still very much on my mind.

Once we got out on the practice range, Odd told me he was not a *marksman*, certainly not an archer, but claimed he was eager to try. He selected his bow. I handed him the quiver full of arrows. The targets were at various distances. The point was to shoot and talk. Take as much time as he liked. I shot first, and let him talk.

"On the 13th of last September, Giuliana and I went in to read the Art Gallery," he said.

"To read?"

---

7   The Gallery featured an exhibit of mostly surrealist paintings.

8   Inspired by the work of M.C. Escher.

"Marshall McLuhan used to say that *reading* is a form of *guessing*. Our guesses and *supposes* pulled us into the paintings we were trying to *read*, if you get me."

"Reading the paintings?" I asked and hit the target.

"That's how I understand it," he said, admiring my skill.

"Well?"

"Well, silence rained down on us as we read the gallery. I understood, reasonably, it was about the artist's inspiration and the theory and practice of art, perhaps, Surrealism and its relation to sex. I also understood that the tour was about us in some strange (is that the right word?) way. Was it not the word that Giuliana liked to use: *strange* as in *odd*? Yet Giuliana did not like what she heard. When I said I didn't know what to say, Giuliana, the true Reader of the Gallery, broke out with: 'What else is there to say, Marath? You've left me no choice,' she added. With her golden eyes and hands of chrome, she closed and locked the Gallery doors and walked away. When I couldn't get out, I began again. 'Don't worry, Marath,' I said aloud. 'This time, you have to *read* the Gallery alone.' So, it became guesses and supposes I wasn't used to, but as in art, so, too, in love, Dr. Wango. Well, have I told you everything you wanted to hear?"

"Yes, you've told me *everything* and *nothing*. But you said *Marath*. You referred to Marath, and not Dylan or Odd, as they call you."

What was his story? What was he about? What was up with this *Dylan* Hedley (alias Odd) business, anyway, and what was he up to, when his real name was likely *Marath*? I was curious. His "tale" was symbolic, allusive, and evasive. So, he "read" the gallery, likely of surrealist paintings, and drew parallels between his experience in that *gallery* (fabricated or real) and his love affair with Giuliana. So what? More relevant was the name switch.

"*Dylan* is a pseudonym, a *nom de guerre*," he said as we shot our arrows. "I adopted it once I came to Canada. And of course, Giuliana calls me *Odd* for reasons of her own."

"Do you want me to call you *Marath*?"

"No, no… not yet," he said angrily. "It's not yet time for the reveal."

"All right," I said to him. "Good, well, let's see how we've done with the targets."

I left him, saying I'd see him later on. As it was, I usually went on very little sleep. Zoo had his theories about my sleeplessness: a doctor and drugs, a doctor with drugs, a doctor on drugs. That was the essence of his theory. Since all I needed was just a little nap, I got a little rest. I'd planned a group activity with my guests. I had some info but needed more for the group fiction, both the study and the case. But something would eventually come out. Something would happen.

That evening, I'd got them playing cards. The house always lost because I put up all the stakes. That was how it was. That was the way I was then, and the way I wanted it to be. Yes, I paid for information. I decided to let Arjuna Sar, the Porter, do what he had been dying to do since first coming here: *talk*. Therefore, I let him talk about what gave him the most pleasure: himself.

"I won't begin with my childhood," he said, "that's been done, but start with my bewilderingly rebellious years at age twenty-one. My mother said to me: 'Marath, most of your brothers and sisters believe they live in a house designed by an architect obsessed with endless stairs.'"

"Marath? Sorry for interrupting, but you distinctly said *Marath*, and not Arjuna."

"*Arjuna* is my own invention. My real name is Marath."

Him too? What was up? Was it a code name? This smacked of conspiracy. Were they conspiring, he and the other Marath, a.k.a. Dylan or Odd? If so, what was their aim?

"Go on," I encouraged him.

"For my rebellion, the only stipulation was that I had to take my mother and my youngest sister with me to a new land. 'I'll take care of the rest,' my father said. Where was I going? 'Where you will start a new life,' he said, 'crossing a new frontier and crossing new borders.'"

Throughout, he was playing his hands and winning.

"Thank you," I said to him.

"But I'm not finished," he said.

"I've heard what I wanted (and needed) to hear. Shall I call you Marath from now on?"

"No, call me Arjuna. I'm not ready to let the others know who I am just yet," he said. "Is that strange?"

"Not particularly," I said, "who is ever ready to do *that*?"

4
MOCKING DOCTORS

At the card game, Professor Athena Headborn appeared to be enjoying herself. She seemed bemused, amused at the tension flaring up between Professor Riddley Hodder and Dr. Bongo Scully. They were playing cards and shouting abuse at each other. This was for the benefit of Athena, who was acting like a smart-alecky referee. When she flashed her eyes up, I realized what (or should I say who?) the source of the trouble was. The instigator was Zoo. He was getting a big kick out of mocking and baiting *the doctors*, as he called them, and flirting aggressively with Athena. He was mocking *doctors*, or *mock-doctors*, as he said. In other words: *quacks*. When I approached, he said,

"And here's another doc. I've got my own college of physicians."

"I'm not a medical doctor," Professor Hodder said.

"Too bad for you, but good for the medical profession," Zoo said.

"Neither am I," Athena said.

"Their loss is our gain, that is if you're playing doctor."

"I bet you want to play doctor," Doctor Bongo Scully said.

"Aren't you doing that already?"

I had a little surprise for them all. I'd invited Doctor Schlangenkopf to attend the session. As if on cue, she strode into the room.

"Whoa," Zoo said. "If she's a doctor, I'm *sick*."

Stunning, she was tall, fair, and imperious.

"I could tell you were ill from the doorway," she said. "But the illnesses I'm interested in are of a different kind altogether."

"Anything good or bad you can say about me is true," Zoo said.

"She's not interested in the lame brain of a carnival freak," Professor Hodder said.

"This lame brain needs a good drain," Zoo said.

"Book in at the Wellness Centre North of Lake Superior," Dr. S. said.

"He already thinks he's superior," Dr. Scully said. "All he has to do is jump in the lake."

It was a nasty crack, but I implored Zoo not to respond and to let it go until later. He said that Dr. Schlangenkopf was sleek and sensuous as a snake. Then smiled. His smile looked like a gash in his face. He'd get back at Doc Bongo, as he was calling him, in his own good time.

With the arrival of Dr. Schlangenkopf the card game came to an abrupt (though indeterminate) end. She had treated Giuliana and knew more than anyone about her case. I told my guests that after dinner and around midnight there would be a pyrotechnic display on the lawn for a bit of amusement.

"What's the celebration?" Professor Hodder asked.

"Wellness," Dr. S. said. "Dr. Wango wants to celebrate the discovery of the secret that lies at the heart of what he calls the group fiction. We are all in that group, am I right, doctor?"

I nodded assent, in awe of her.

"So, he is convinced that during dinner the puzzle will be solved and we can celebrate the fact with fireworks at midnight."

"An excuse for telling tales," Arjuna said, "and following it up with a good bang."

"I can't think of a better excuse," I suggested, "unless excusing yourself to go the toilet."

"Make-believe and storytelling as evidence?"

"Fact and fiction, yes, the interplay, the byplay, the play."

"The feel of the real," Odd said.

At that point, Professor Brainerd joined us, and so did Giuliana. Both Maraths (Odd and Arjuna to distinguish them) stood side by side. Upon seeing her therapist, Giuliana stopped dead in her tracks.

"Dr. Schlangenkopf," she whispered.

"Dinner?" asked Professor Brainerd. "Good. I've worked up an appetite. When do we eat?"

"Soon," I said. "But there are ground rules for the dining experience at all my Truth Parties. For this one, it must be agreed upon that you will submit to hypnosis conducted by Dr. S. so that we can free the mind and tongue to let the stories come out without conscious distortion. Are you game? I know you must have questions. You are all *questioners*, as it were, but we must leave the questions to the dinner."

"Under hypnosis? How do we eat?"

"As you usually do," Dr. S. said, according to our pre-arranged plan. "The process will not obstruct your enjoyment of the meal. Dr. Wango assures me it is sumptuous."

"Oh, yes," I said. "I'm famous for my dinner parties."

"Truth parties," Zoo said. "You should have been here for the last one."

"Truth parties…"

"What exactly are you looking for?" Odd asked. "What kind of truth?"

"Trace evidence."

"Of what? Bloodstains."

"Maybe, and maybe conspiracy or the workings of a secret society, or how the 'beheading' actually came about, and what it really signifies. But the reason for hypnosis is that I have heard some of your versions of events and your descriptions of situations in your lives, and since you are all good with words, bookish, academic, you know all about interlacing narratives, and all about Scheherazade in *One Thousand and One Nights,* telling tales to save her life, and all about Boccaccio's *Decameron* with its stories told to escape the plague, and you know all about Chaucer's *Canterbury Tales* told by pilgrims on the pilgrimage, and likely even know about Italo Calvino's *If on a Winter's Night a Traveller,* a book about the art of telling tales in which 'you' are the main character; and since our friends here know about the 'curative' power of books and ideas, they know the so-called 'willing suspension of disbelief' and the 'literal-metaphorical' interpretation of everything from the Bible to graphic novels, and know and likely study and/or teach the notion of 'balance' and 'imbalance' as artists such as storytellers oppose the culture that breeds insanity, and helps to cure it of sickness. But for you people, words can also deceive, used consciously as you use them, or lead to obfuscation if not intended for the truth. This makes it necessary to go deeper, to listen to your unconscious language, the dream language, for the sake of determining what is going on in this group."

"Hypnotize me," Professor Athena Headborn said. "I'm in."

"If she's in, I'm in," said Dr. Bongo Scully.

"If he's in because she's in, then I'm in to protect her from him," Professor Ridley Hodder said, trying not to mean it.

"Not the first time for me," Giuliana said. "I know the hypnotist personally."

"I don't, but I'm curious," Odd said.

"My curiosity is greater," Arjuna said, humourlessly.

"I'm not a part of this story," Zoo said, "but I'm interested in seeing everybody going under."

"Will you be going under Dr. Wango?"

"Only if Dr. Schlangenkopf wants me to."

"I do."

"Hypnotize me," I said. "I'll try not to resist suggestion."

"I'll work on each of you," Dr. S. said, "as a preliminary, and then get you together at dinner to do the collective part of the hypnosis."

She sent us off to prepare ourselves. We had to *undress* for dinner. She'd meet us in our bedrooms to get things started. If the meetings with my guests were anything like her meeting with me, it'd go well for the most part and would result in agreeing to arrive at the dinner table totally naked. What she didn't tell us was that the dinner would be a totally nude affair, a full frontal display. We'd be undressing soon.

Just how Dr. S. managed to convince us to strip and discard our clothing, especially for a dinner party, was a credit to her mysterious ways and persuasive powers. It had something to do with her talk of wellness, and maybe the directness of her remarkably luminous eyes.

She was naked, gloriously so, when she led the group in to the dining room. Zoo had willingly stripped. What was he doing here? Why hadn't he gone about his business? We'd accepted his presence as part of the seeking of truth among us, at our own peril.

Giuliana stood apart at first, trying to look self-assured. But Professor Athena looked perfectly comfortable in her skin. Dr. Bongo was strikingly handsome in the raw. But Professor Hodder was covering his privates with both hands. He was covered in sores and welts. Something was being settled between them. Professor Brainerd was muscular for an older man, proud of his nudity. Odd was not. He was furtive, almost shy, but in an aggressive way. Arjuna kept bowing as if in a ceremony to show us his backside. He also spun like a dervish. I was already seated.

Only candlelight as required by Dr. S. illuminated the table. It looked as if she were a medium presiding over an séance. She had been speaking since she'd first entered the room. Her words were soothing, comforting, but veiled. We were all seated now. Dinner commenced. She looked directly at Odd. He was already talking. He said what sounded like this:

"An old hag adopted me. I was the bastard son of her friend, Arruna."

"Arjuna?" I asked, seeking clarification.

"No, Arruna," he said. "This Arruna character was a pathetic whore, but connected to some rich idiot. That's not all. She had shot one of her johns or lovers some years ago. Arruna took me to see her lying in prison, dying. What was I doing there? This woman was my mother. And I soon realized she'd killed my father. Years go by. I'm grown up now, working as a maker of instruments, mostly violins. On a delivery of one of my creations, I met a revolutionary. His name was Marath. He got me involved in his brand of radical politics. He was hooked up with a beautiful but crazy bitch. I realized we had something in common. I was seeing a woman out of her head most of the time, vulgar, arrogant. One night, we went to see a concert. It was there I met Athena, getting away from those chasing after her. I was smitten, infatuated, possessed. You can see why. She's intelligent, beautiful, and not crazy. Turns out she's a radical herself, though teaching at the university, and living away from the men that she has *fascinated*. They bore her. That includes the two doctors, one medical, one not. Under her influence, I accepted a plan to carry out an assassination. I didn't know who the intended target was. I visited her. Ask her. She'll tell you. And I told her everything I knew about my folks. She let me into her life, and not only her life. I had to get back home because the woman who'd adopted me was dying. I tried to be of some comfort to her in her last moments. She left me an inheritance. It was nothing much but more than I had. My life took a turn. I got into crime, drugs, sex, but I was no longer interested in politics or revolutions. Athena, however, reminded me of my *obligation* to carry out the killing. But when the time came for me to shoot, I turned the gun on myself, and shot point blank."

But why wasn't he dead? Had he beaten the hypnosis in order to trick us with a lie? As if she had heard my thought, Dr. S. stared at him and then began watching Odd. He ate his meal with relish. Dr. Athena opened her mouth, but soon closed it, thinking better of speaking now.

Were we really in a trance? I mean, we were naked, but were we hypnotized? Then Professor Brainerd spoke as though from the other room with such a distant and gloomy voice, it made you think he was dead and speaking from beyond the grave. I mean, we knew he was not decapitated. Yes, it was a serious injury, but not a beheading. So, did his story have symbolic value only? Now what was he trying to say? Unbidden, he spoke. Professor Brainerd started right in with:

"During my hospital stay. I couldn't keep still. I felt a strong desire to wander, to see who else was there, to look in on the other patients, and to see suffering first-hand. It was on my tour, making my rounds, as it were, before the nurses hustled me back to my room and into my bed that I saw one of my students, Giuliana Koffmann. She had been there on the day of my 'decapitation' as I was calling it. She had seen me lose my head, and I suppose she had lost hers, but only in another sense. When we got together, I told Giuliana I wanted to know more about her. She had a look of horror in her eyes, as if seeing one of the undead, which in a sense I suppose I was: back from the dead, I mean, well, not exactly, but given a second chance to live. I wanted her to call me by my name, Karl, so that she would be less intimidated, less threatened by her philosophy professor standing in front of her or sitting by her hospital bed in his hospital gown, clutching his head with one hand and holding onto the IV pole with the other. I asked her if we could talk. She said she'd think about it. On the cusp of getting *intimate*, of getting to know her away from the class, Giuliana told me things about herself in connection to her family. Since there was pain in her account, I seemed to be particularly interested in her story. Suffering piqued my curiosity. But just as quickly, I lost interest in it. As if part of my second chance at life with a new attitude, I turned my attention to myself, to my head, as it were. One way or another, my life has always been about my head."

"It should be cut off," Odd said. "Oh, wait, we already tried that."

"Funny, your head should be cut off."

"All right, should I do it, or will you do the honours?"

"No more talk of heads and decapitations."

Professor Brainerd was continuing to eat and drink with no visible signs of anxiety, completely relaxed, gregarious, and not a human attraction or human oddity as at a freak show, the man who had once lost his head.

Dr. S. furrowed her brow. Why was she not eating? Well, yes, she was conducting this experiment, but was apparently not buying what was being said. The nudity was more a reflection of her than it was of us. Perhaps, she was a nudist. She was a strikingly beautiful human being. No one spoke for a while. I heard the sound of plates, forks, spoons, knives, glass… chewing, sipping. Then:

"I think it has to do with my sister, Giuliana," said Professor Athena Headborn.

All sounds ceased. Everyone lowered his or her head as if in prayer, as if on cue. We were in a trance all right. The hypnosis had kicked in. Or had it?

"Surprise," she said, "but she's the baby in the family, and never wants me to acknowledge her. But without a stitch on, I can say what I like, and what I like is to say that she must learn to live without blaming everyone for her unhappiness. It must be like leaving December forever, for a chance at a new life in a new year. This time, she'll know happiness."

"Does she?"

"What?"

"Know happiness?"

"No happiness, I'm afraid, as you yourself know from treating her at the Wellness Centre, am I right?"

"Or are you wrong?"

"I'm right."

"As always?"

"As always."

Then my guests seemed to be asleep, falling into a trance-like state, nodding off, but not all at the same time.

5
THE CARNIVAL OF HUMAN ATTRACTIONS

Dr. S. wasn't saying much, if anything at all. When she spoke, it seemed to be less than she already knew. Then she stepped it up with provocations and sticking barbs into her comments ready to pluck out our eyes.

"You're in love, aren't you, Professor Headborn?"

"Am I in love? Is that what you want to know? Yes, I suppose I am."

"It's not the one we suppose it is, is it?"

"Not the one you suppose? What's your supposition?"

"I could say Professor Hodder."

"You could."

"But it wouldn't be him."

"It wouldn't?"

"No… and I suppose I could say Dr. Bongo Scully."

"Why him?"

"Exactly, because they both think they have a chance with you. So who is your lover?"

"Who?"

"I am," said Professor Brainerd, as if coming to from a deep sleep.

The others laughed. Athena did, too, and then stopped before the others did.

"It's Karl, isn't it?"

"Karl? Professor Brainerd. Yes, I've been in love with him since grad school. I took a course with him, and was smitten, and have been ever since."

Dr. Bongo Scully made what sounded like animal noises, the sounds of jealousy. Professor Hodder squealed in a high-pitched voice; a dying insect. They were sad men, thwarted in love. Wronged.

Then Dr. S. opened her arms as if to embrace them. She closed her eyes. She looked like a high priestess of some cult. Everybody spoke at once. I tried to piece it together, this inchoate, cacophonous, choral work. It was like a lost language, a dream language. To understand it, you needed to decipher the code of its lost alphabet. As I heard it, much to Dr. S.'s delight, I said it aloud.

"That is my story," Arjuna bawled out. "*My* story, do you hear me? It is the story of my life. You stole it… the way it was between Giuliana and me, yes, the Porter. Did I not have a right to enjoy myself with a student? I took up with her. I pleased her. I pleasured her."

"Liar," Odd said. "That is my story."

"These stories belong to all of you," Dr. S. interjected, "and to no one, for they are *stolen*. You have misappropriated them."

"False?" I asked.

"False as water," she said. "Don't you recognize them?"

"Patterns, archetypes?"

"Thefts," she insisted. "These are people made up entirely of words. Language is their refuge. They plagiarize everything, unless they have to cite their sources. As academics, they lie with impunity until they are caught."

"You have caught them?"

"I've caught them. Of course, I have had a head start. I've treated Giuliana before, and know Professor Headborn. Odd's story, for instance…"

"Yes, all right, I made it up," he confessed.

"No, you swiped it," Arjuna said.

"The source of his story is one by the American novelist, Henry James. I think it is based on *The Princess Casamassima*."

"It makes for a good story," Odd said, "even now with a few changes to character and plot."

"But it is not the story of your life. Still, it speaks volumes about you and your secret identity, your self-concept, if you will, and the mystery that you are living, especially in reference to anarchists and revolutionaries."

"If they are not original stories, whose are they?" I asked.

"Does it matter?" Dr. S. replied. "This is not a seminar in one of the professors' courses. But for your sake, let me say that most of the tales come from a book written by a failed writer. He did research on these subjects and wrote a collection that he linked to myth, called *The Pros and Cons of Dragon Slaying*."

"Then what has been gained?"

"A glimpse into their imaginative lives," she said. "They are naked."

"We're naked. How did you get us to strip?"

"I didn't."

"But we are, as you say, naked."

"You wanted to be."

"A group of academics finally gets what it wants. Dr. Bongo wanted it too, and Zoo was already half-naked, I believe, before I came."

"Got what we wanted?"

"To see each other naked."

"Like in the sixties?"

"The Sixties got a lot wrong, but one thing it got right: it's about getting naked."

"Right on."

"Are we hypnotized at all?"

"Can't say for sure; maybe, maybe not."

As if they suddenly became aware of their nudity with its beauty and vulgarity, they began to agitate, squirm, writhe, looking for a way out of this situation.

"What was the point? To delay? To postpone? To discover or uncover something about us?"

"Yes, all of the above, especially in light of the 'beheading' and what really happened. You are tied together, like a group of characters in a play or a story, by the professor's losing his head. You saw a man carrying his head, but more than that, there are jealousies here. You envy each other. You bargain with reality to get the upper hand in your dealings with one other."

"For instance?"

"One of the reference points in this group is Giuliana. She breaks your heart. She's so talented, but so lost. She doesn't know how to choose men, how to be with them, how to stay with them."

"Or anybody else."

"Nobody stays with her. She renounces her talents, gives up her gifts, and turns on herself and others."

"Sad, sad, sad, the one who will always be sad, wronged, broken-hearted, the one left behind. Everybody wants her. Nobody fulfills her or cares for her in the way she wants."

"I care."

"No, you don't. You couldn't be happy with me, and that's what happened."

"There are other instances."

"Well?"

"The use of the name *Marath*."

"That's my real name," Odd said. "All right, I've said it."

"It isn't your real name," Arjuna said. "It's mine."

"No, it is a code name."

"Code? For what?"

"A secret society?"

"A conspiracy."

"They're conspirators? They hate each other."

"They know each other well."

"Nonsense, Dr. S. If you are a doctor, you're spewing absolute crap."

"Don't speak to her that way," Giuliana said. "I'll kill you."

"You're up to something," Zoo said.

With deft and quick moves, Arjuna and Odd lunged for him. They might be naked, but they were suddenly armed with knives and forks, dinner hardly touched. The attack seemed coordinated, planned. Zoo, though unprepared for this battle, delighted in the confrontation, and resisted with the strength of a much younger man.

"What's happening?"

"An attempt on his life."

Dr. S. said a word that sounded like *Marath*. They immediately let go, and then ran off.

"Where are they going?"

"Where I sent them: to their rooms. The co-conspirators jumped the gun. They missed their intended target."

"Him? Why him?"

"Not *him*. Professor Brainerd, and, well, we shall see who the real target is tonight."

"At the fireworks?"

"With a bang, we'll know everything. All will be revealed in the glow of the pyrotechnic display."

"Hooray."

We were sent off to dress. But Professor Brainerd alone sat eating his meal in peace. That is, relative peace. He had escaped an attempt. I hurried along to catch up to Odd and Arjuna. What was their story?

6
MYSTIFICATION AND DEMYSTIFICATION

They were lying naked together on the bed in the guest room assigned to Arjuna. They were in a trancelike state. Dr. S.'s *hocus-pocus* (or auto-suggestion) seemed finally to have kicked in. I could have sworn I heard one of them say (or was it in unison?):

"Sometimes, you have to sleep with the enemy."

With very little prompting, they spoke almost as one person, slowing down, speeding up, their voices sounding similar as they told me what they wanted me to know.

"It was like dying and being reborn."

"Everything back home had seemed apocalyptic."

"So, it was inevitable that we had to escape."

"As a refugee, two atmospheres were just right for a documentary filmmaker like me."

"Like *me*."

"Leaving the island nation, I went missing."

"I went missing."

"The authorities found us, rescued us, held us and kept us."

"While we waited for the claim of refugee status to go through, they housed us in the detention centre in Vancouver."

"In a series of interrogations, we were held for two months and then, like rebirth, we were sent out East and settled in Toronto."

"Free."

"We were free."

Dr. S. was not far away, but actually very nearby. I knew she had been listening in on this: two men telling the same story, and believing they were, in fact, the same man. Who did they think they were? What was this: the *Tweedledee and Tweedledum* syndrome? I'd known it for quite some time that the psychotherapist had allowed this interweaving of narratives to go on for her own purposes. It was her move, as far as I was concerned, and up to her to call it. I wasn't the referee, the umpire, or the controller. She was.

"Stop right there," Dr. S. blurted out, invading the room.

"Why stop them now?"

"They're telling the same tale."

"I figured as much."

"They think they're the same person with the identical histories."

"Well… and so?"

"They may be, but the story they're telling as if they've lived it out as one man is not *their* story."

"Whose is it?"

"Ask them—these conjoined twins. Or him… if they prefer."

I asked the question and without skipping a beat the two acting as one said:

"Discovered."

"The story is found in a notebook I collected some years ago: *The Pros & Cons of Dragon Slaying*."

"Is this true?" I asked them.

"True."

"True."

"It's as true as any fiction and as any story will allow. You can check their words against the source."

"So they're actors, readers…"

"Liars," she said, and ordered them to go to bed and get some rest.

"I'll deal with you later," she insisted, despite their derisive laughter.

"I hope so," one of them said.

"Ditto," said the other.

They did as she said. I could hear their threatening laughter.

"The others are having a good laugh, too," she said.

"At my expense? Or yours? Or ours"

"Sometimes mine, sometimes yours."

"What do we know then, Dr. S.?"

"We know what can be known."

"They're planning something, am I right?"

"Yes, so are the others."

"Are they all conspirators?"

"Yes, conspiring against each other, and maybe one of us. What we are witnessing are the public dreams of anarchists."

"Shall I go ahead with the planned fireworks, or do we have a plenary session with these deceivers, liars, conspirators to get things out in the open?"

"Pyrotechnics as planned," she said.

"The Truth Party *after*, eh? It's not the usual order for me."

"It is for me."

"And so, just for you, the Truth Party after the firecrackers it will be."

PART TWO

Human Attractions & Human Oddities

1
TRUTH CRIMES

"You think the world is made up of literature. You think reality is a
piece of paper."
—From *The Messiah of Stockholm* by Cynthia Ozick

It had started with a whimper, and it would end with a bang, or the
other way around. It all seemed like a translation from another story
in a completely different language. Or better, an approximation of
reality.

I was asking, I was *just* asking: "Is midnight all right?"

"For what?" Zoo wanted to know.

"For cleaning up a mess," I darkly whispered.

"A mess is a mess," he said, "as you well know from your work here,
but what kind of mess are you talking?"

"Well, as I read it, and have come to understand it, Dr. Schlangenkopf
had double-booked the end of the session," I said, as if in a trance, or
just coming to. "That made a fine mess of the mess we were in. It was
up to me to clean it up."

"It was dirty? The end, I mean."

"It was filthy, because somebody shat the bed hard."

"Who?"

"That's what I'm itching to find out."

Professor Brainerd was there, just arrived, and overheard our palaver.

"I recollect the kind of mess the leader of the commune I stayed at once referred to as the ritualizing of the end of days."

"When was that?"

"In my time with my ma and a man named Fernando Strange," he said. "It was on the west coast, the compound. I've always wondered what I've kept from that time? Maybe, the notion of an end point, daily rites rooted in parables and superstitions. But I was a teenage alcoholic thanks to it all: the doom saying, threats, allegations, veiled violence, expectations, hippie thinking, and free love that was never free. Then I had turned to drugs and was an addict. I found sobriety in my early twenties, or it found me in the form of Val Wix, a true lover, and I became a smoker, and then just started vaping to rid myself of all habits. Still, I set fire to each bed I slept in, as I was instructed to do, a new bed each night in the wilderness, kicking over the traces. I burned my beds and those of others, especially Val's. Thin-skinned, I remembered all the reprimands, the laying on of hands, the rough kisses and burns, and unkind words, the nudity. I was still sensitive to code words such as blind allegiance. I didn't want to control anybody. I believed that nobody had the right to control me: no person, organization, or government. 'Don't ask me for self-sacrifice,' I used to say when cornered. Shiftless upon leaving the commune, I drifted, and made drifting a way of life. I soon lost all my maps, the one I was given, and the ones I had made. They got me nowhere fast but here. I hated the idea of *You are here*. Fernando Strange had taught me that. He wasn't even wrong. I don't want to control anybody or any choice. I don't even want to control myself. About most things, I'm seldom right."

"Who is?" I asked.

"'You're right, you're right,' Fernando Strange used to say before he disciplined me. 'But not as right as you are wrong.' Then I travelled all the time from coast to coast. I still like the ocean—Pacific or Atlantic, I don't mind as long as I can stand in the water and look out. I like doing it for hours, the waves rolling against me. For some, all the moving was as hard as moving from the East coast to the hinterland or leaving the North to live in the South. That was Val. I had to leave her. It wasn't as hard as it seemed. I wasn't a pick-up artist, as they used to say, but I was somebody women picked up. I guess, I picked up with whoever was there looking back at me staring hard at them."

"Who was there?"

"Athena, for one. They had said I was insane for trying to get out. Madness was a drug even then. It kept me going. It gave me edge. As I thought about it, it hadn't been hard to escape. Perhaps, Fernando Strange had wanted it that way. It was easy, too easy, to get away from the past. Why? To lure me back, what else? Was it to draw me back to the place, as if of my own free will? Was it to control me after years of no contact, as if flicking a switch, or pulling an invisible lever? Mind control, as they used to say. I swore I'd never return. But then, my ma was still there. I don't know how her phone call reached me on the beach. The maternal force always drew me back. He has his agents."

"Who?"

"Fernando Strange."

"Who's working for him?"

"Athena, for one, and that Schlangenkopf woman, the so-called psycho-therapist from up North."

"You don't trust her?"

"Not as far as I can get away from her."

"You want to get away from me again?" asked Dr. S., sidling up to us. She was always around, coming out of nowhere, mostly the shadows, appearing.

"Do you see what I mean?" Professor Brainerd asked, as if we could. "Hard to get away, can't get away from such a force, eternally present with the futility of trying to escape, but there are ways."

"Are there? What ways?"

"We'll make another attempt soon enough, but not now, not with the hospitality of Dr. Wango, and besides, I can't remember why I'm here."

"The beheading story," Dr. S. reminded him. "The corresponding stories of the witnesses: the real reason is to clear up the mystery that binds us together."

"Save it for after the fireworks," he said. "We are having a bonfire, aren't we?"

"As promised," I reassured him.

"Our own Gunpowder Plot... our own Guy Fawkes Day... let's hope this one turns out."

He left us to ourselves and went in to prepare for the evening. I reminded him that the fireworks began at midnight. He kept his back to us and waved both hands in the air. I thought I heard him saying:

"Bang, bang, boom, boom, whiz-bang!" But I was likely wrong. The Italian company I'd hired to do the fireworks were specialists, usually doing weddings, or contests, or even New Years celebrations or Canada Day or Fourth of July. They'd been at it for days setting up their frames for the pyrotechnics. Should be quite a bang and boom.

I asked Dr. S. to confer with me on the case so far.

"What will be the great reveal?" I asked.

"Maybe, that there is nothing to reveal," she said.

"So far, they've all been lying to us... to each other..."

"And to themselves."

"What about *us*?"

"What *about* us?"

"Are we lying? Have we been lying?"

"Well, only in the service of the truth."

"What is that truth, Dr. S., according to you?"

"I have no story but the one encyclopaedic story of my clients and patients. I have no life but theirs, or outside their pain. Their wellbeing is my wellbeing. When they are not there... well, I don't exist."

"You need them, then, to survive."

"To breathe, to live."

"To dream about? To fantasize?"

"To keep them? Is that what you're saying?"

"To find them, hold them, keep them."

"I suppose... if that's what works for you."

"What works for you? Compassion?"

"Compassion kills, Dr. Wango. I want them to see the futility of pity. The talking cure or the love cure, as Freud himself confessed, makes psychotherapy a cure through love."

"Dangerous liaisons, for sure."

"Transference, you mean, and counter-transference."

"Attraction that one feels for the doctor."

"And the doctor feels for the patient."

"Is there a cure?"

"If you believe in miracles."

"The miracle of a change of outlook, a change of heart... a transformation, I guess, but not the speeding up or slowing down of natural laws... no, not magic, but the miraculous."

"And yet, some are cured by love."

"Not alone by *love*."

"Not alone."

"Your method is risky, isn't it?"

"I take the risk."

"Your patients have been using stories, which you've identified, but perhaps those stories symbolize something for them… perhaps, the telling of those tales speaks volumes for them."

"Yes, perhaps, but psychotherapy is not literary criticism."

"But there is love and interpretation in both."

"You are a lover and interpreter of human oddities," Luna said.

"Of human attractions," I qualified, finding I was breathing a little quicker at her expression.

"You're involved either way," she said.

"And you? What's your personal involvement with these people? For instance, you've been treating Giuliana…"

"Yes, treating, not *mistreating*. And I've… connected with the others: Brainerd, Headborn, Hodder and Scully. The thing that binds them is…"

"The head," I whispered. "The story of the 'beheading' and their names… all relating to the head in some way."

"Well, yes, but is that coincidence or correlation?"

"On the level of language, maybe coincidence, but on the level of myth, irony, symbol, deeper and deeper."

"What about Odd?"

"Hedley," I said.

"Arjuna?"

"The exception, but he identifies with this Odd to the point where one is indistinguishable from the other… or he wants to be one with him… a conjoined twin… connected at the head… one brain…"

How far could we get with this line of reasoning… this speculation and freewheeling thinking? We couldn't get far, though it was kind of fun, but as far as we could get was never figured out, because somebody was shouting blue murder within our earshot. It was Zoo.

"They're killing each other," he said.

"Who?"

Before he answered, he pointed in the direction of what looked like a schoolyard fight spilling onto the lawn. Dr. Bongo was doing battle with Professor Hodder. It was a pitched battle with no quarter given. The combatants tore at each other and fought on. The others were shouting at them with Giuliana calling them names, Professor Brainerd laughing hysterically, Professor Athena Headborn studying the fighters with keen interest, and Odd and Arjuna placing bets. The combatants were standing face-to-face, trading punches, or wildly flailing their arms with plenty of pushing and shoving going on.

"Why are they fighting, and what for?"

"They're fighting over me," Professor Headborn said.

"Or about something I said," Zoo said.

"What did you say?"

"Well, I suggested that a barroom brawl between two doctors is something I'd lay money on."

"This is regressive behaviour… they've likely never been in a fist fight in all their lives… lives of privilege and entitlement…"

"Split them up," I demanded. "Intervene before somebody gets hurt."

Bongo came out hard. Hodder got hurt. Bongo went harder. A horrifying scene. Bongo punched Hodder till he went slack. Then Hodder was bent backwards. Bongo kept punching like a machine at the partly awake Hodder. It was hard to watch. Blows crashed down onto the body going limp in front of Bongo.

It got worse. Three times the others picked Hodder up off the grass, revived him, and then began the standing count. The fight continued. Hodder got every break he deserved, and then some, but Bongo beat him stone cold. It was a shocking punishment that Bongo unleashed on the university professor that was obviously not a fighter, but an aesthete.

Professor Headborn shouted that she'd fight the winner of the Bongo-Hodder bout. She watched the fight closely. Then she decided she'd have no part of a Bongo match. She jumped in between the fighters. They embraced her and wrestled to the ground. The others got involved. They were tumbling together with Zoo laughing his cruel ass off.

On my order, with the assistance of Zoo and Dr. S. (she was remarkably strong), the crazed combatants parted. They sat on the lawn, winded, surrounded.

"I'll square them," Dr. S. said, tending to their wounds, cuts, abrasions, bruises and contusions.

"No, I'll square them," said professor Athena Headborn, thrusting forward. "I'm the straightener, and I'll straighten them out."

"The truth is: don't say or do anything you'll live to regret," Professor

Brainerd interjected.

"No regret is the truth," she said.

"What truth?" shouted Bongo.

"You lead us on," Hodder added. "You have us, but don't know what to do with us."

"I'm not leading anyone on," she replied, "or having or not having."

"You make us believe we have a chance with you," Bongo said.

"You won't stop pestering me," she insisted. "Well, maybe the truth might stop you in your tracks."

"I'll tell it, dear," Professor Brainerd said, sidling up. "Professor Headborn… Athena… and I are married. Secretly married. I'm true to her in our secret arrangement, and she's loyal to me in our relationship."

"You've been deceiving us," Bongo said to Athena.

"You've been deceiving yourselves," she uttered.

"We live as we live for philosophical reasons," said Brainerd. "It's been amusing hiding it from the snoops on campus."

"You're talking about me," suggested Arjuna.

"You, yes, you…. you snoop… you creep in and out of rooms, conversations, lives, and creep out again. You stop me to talk about your so-called philosophical bent… you persecute me with inanities. If you want to talk to me, then take my class."

"The other persecutor is Hodder," said Professor Athena. "Always *coming on* to me, pressuring me, saying he's protecting me when in fact he's patronizing me, harassing me, pursuing me, plaguing me."

"You are a bastard," Professor Brainerd said to Hodder. "You prey on people with your smugness and arrogance, and when they don't agree with you, you challenge them to a fight."

"And lose," said Bongo.

"And lose, for now," said Hodder. "I got drawn in based on a flirtation with Athena."

"I thought you were joking," she said.

"I was at first but then I fell," he said.

"It was Hodder who put me up to insulting Professor Brainerd," Odd said.

"You were good at it," the old prof said.

"At least some things have been squared with a little blood," I said to them, noting the lateness of the hour with the fireworks set to go off at midnight.

"Nothing's been squared," said Giuliana.

"I agree," said Zoo. "From my vantage point, it is all just a shaggy dog story filled with absurdities, nothings, cheats."

"Nothing but hurt," said Giuliana and took off screaming.

"Giuliana. She'll get hurt, hurt somebody, or hurt herself."

"Where is she going?"

"She's off and running."

"Often running off."

2
THE GREAT REVEAL

The answer to Dr. Scully's question was: *The Maze*. Giuliana was heading right for it. We all gave chase. The maze in daylight was one thing, but at night, still another, and a potential disaster for a crazed person running through it, lost, lost, lost, to the point of despair of ever getting out.

"She's been in a lot of stories," said Dr. S., "as it were, in her life, and now she's in an escape story—her own."

"The maze is treacherous at night," I said. "Not all should enter in pursuit."

It was too late. Zoo was in, and so were the other fools. Dr. S. and I did not venture in. Shouts, warnings, appeals, everybody was calling to everybody else.

"Take my hand," I said to Dr. S., "or stay out."

She was on the point now of going in, but hesitated again, thinking better of it. She took my hand, and then my arm.

More screaming. The pyrotechnics had begun.

"Who? Who knows the way out of the maze?"

"We're under attack," shouted Zoo, running back out to confront us.

He was having a ball.

"This is what comes of stories," he shouted, as if on an outdoor stage.

Soon with the blast of fireworks we wouldn't be able to hear him at all.

"Your storytelling... even the great stories are a muddle. You can't tell it straight... so you invent and twist and manipulate... even the funny ones deceive, betray. Your stories have led to this coil. Who loves whom? Who did what to whom? Who's wrong? Who's right... in a maze of Arabian Nights... stories you think will help you to survive... but they kill... they kill the truth... the desire... the meaning... all so clever with plot and characters and mystery and so-called action, but nobody goes anywhere... sitting in a chair... nobody does anything with stories... they're just words... doing nothing or going nowhere fast... while you're sitting still... or standing or lying down?"

"That's the point," Dr. S. shouted back.

"What point? What point are you making? What point is it possible for you to make that isn't self-serving?"

"The point is this: stories make us vulnerable and keep us human. Our stories tie us together."

"If I thought that," Zoo spat out, "I'd kill myself... or you."

"You'd go that far?" she asked him.

"Later," he said. "I've got to get our flight risk out of the maze. Her attitude is *weaponized*."

He let us have it bang in our faces. Bang went the fireworks. Midnight, as planned, had arrived with gunpowder. Boom. Boom.

"He loves to quarrel when he's not seducing somebody," I said to Dr. S. as loudly as I could over the explosions.

"He's going in after her."

"We'll go in after him."

"No, let's stay here, Dr. Wango."

"And watch the fireworks?"

"And watch the fireworks... come what may."

"When sorrows come, I hear, and they will..."

"And they do, dear doctor."

"Right, in battalions, as always, not single spies."

"Do you mean for those lost in the labyrinth?"

"In the maze... amazed by now at how easy it is to get lost with the night sky lit up with bombardment."

"Will they get lost?"

"One way or the other... and I just sent away the helicopters not a day or so ago, but if I need them for a rescue, I'm sure I can get them back."

"What fireworks!" Dr. S. exclaimed.

"What have we done to them?" I asked her, standing close.

"To our patients? What have we not done, or left undone."

"Ka-boom!"

"Amazing! Imagine what they're seeing scurrying through the maze."

"All in looking up at the fiery sky... in endless explosions."

"They'll have to get together. Pair up. Or regroup to make it out."

"All for Giuliana's sake in running away. She's good at that...

running away, I mean."

"It's a trap."

"We'll wait for the sad parade to find a way out… or go in to them."

I led her to the terrace for a more comfortable view of the pyrotechnics. By comfortable, I mean seated on cushioned and comfy chairs… even the swing was a thought… for more intimate viewing. I offered her a drink from the outside bar. She was all for a brandy. Easy, easy, brandy it was. She looked serene in contrast to the explosive sky. She began musing, no doubt, on those caught in the maze.

"At the best times of our lives, why do the worst things happen?"

"We're better than this, better than our pain, better than the shitload of money we need to get rid of our debts."

"We're better than this… better than the fake tyrants and their trumpy dictatorships…"

"We're better than the conspiracy theories and false allegations."

"What allegations?"

"Of manipulation, of quackery… of depredation… of funking it."

"Psychotherapy, you mean."

"And analysis… and mind control."

"Well, what do you think?"

"About anything in particular?"

"About them—these people that have brought us together only to leave us for the maze."

"What do I think? I think they are not real."

"No, they're not."

"Is it our job to make them so?"

"If we take it on or continue to do so… the job is ours."

"Is reality?"

"Who else can do it?"

"Not the way we can. The rest is madness if we don't."

"What do you suppose they will find in their chase in the depth and darkness of that labyrinth?"

"New alliances, new separations, new treacheries, cowardice or heroism, fear or laughter… they'll find something or be found out."

"Once out, they have to be sounded… we'll sound them… on what they found."

"Is this at all real?"

"Are they real? Very real, I mean, at all?"

"I see what you mean. No, not… not *very*… *not* real at all… at all."

"Incredible designs in the night sky… as real as that."

"As real as the affection I'm feeling for you, dear doctor."

"Call me Clive, Dr. S."

"Call me Luna, Clive."

"Ah, the moon… the goddess of the moon sitting next to me… would you like to swing in the covered swing?"

"I thought you'd never ask."

"So, now."

"Yes?"

"So now what are these folks about… really and truly?"

"Well, really and truly, they are highly educated folks, informed, shaped culturally… but their enthusiasms for things of the mind cannot conceal or help them with their resentments."

"Resentments towards?"

"Reality… each other… themselves… the government… God… name it."

"I'm naming it vicarious or inauthentic… they cannot author their own lives. They live in the stories of others… not just living out a dream or acting one out during sleep… but asleep in somebody else's fantasy… lived out as their own."

"Bang on."

Bang, bang… the fireworks affirmed us.

"I suppose we all take a page out of somebody else's book… in the sense that we imitate others… their life stories… ambitions… struggles… achievements… and borrow or steal a script from those we admire, envy or resent… success and failure are the gambles… rather than writing only after living it… the life we're condemned to… thinking we've chosen it… or the life we chose believing we're damned to make it or lose. It is a life of handicaps… I can't do this… I can't do that… I used to be able to do such and such… but I just can't anymore. Or: I'm sick… or sick to death with trying."

"So the beheading story?"

"Brought these folks together… tied them together… but also tied them up and tied them down."

"There's a plot here, I think, for something is going on… and I can't read it or follow it… like the enforced marriage of different tales."

"All fantasy has broken loose… in all spheres of life… from the constant lies of government officials to the propaganda of self-help… to the veiled threats of extinction… we're living random lives… nothing is what it seems... nothing seems what it is... for my people..."

"Your patients?"

"My patients, yes, they talk themselves into corners."

"I suppose we all do. The trick is to talk yourself out of them."

"Exactly... the talking cure... especially at the Wellness Centre. You must visit me there, Clive."

"I thought you'd never ask."

It was more than flirtation.

"And here," she said, "at the mansion, your approach is a kind of..."

"Play therapy... acting out... with the games and the archery range and the maze and fireworks... play as a form of... love."

I meant it for her. I was falling hard.

"Love? Yes... the love cure... but did it work... or, like the talking cure, did it sometimes go too far?"

A movement frightened me. The fireworks? Maybe, but I didn't get a second to breathe when Dr. S., my dear Luna, screamed out. She was hit...

"I'm shot," she said.

She fell. I tended to her. An arrow pierced her through the shoulder from the front, close to the heart... too close. It was Giuliana that stepped before us with a bow from the archery range and a quiver full of arrows. Her stance was one of determination.

"Traitor," she said. "You betrayed me."

"You escaped the maze," I blurted out. "Put the bow down."

"I never went in deep," she exclaimed. "I hid... remember, you had already taken me before... I knew something those idiots didn't know... how to get out quickly... the secret of the maze."

She put another arrow on the bow... took aim.

"Everything you did, you did against me," Giuliana raved.

I was frantic. Fireworks blinded me. Giuliana stood poised to make a kill. I must help Luna.

"Don't shoot the arrow, Giuliana, I beg you... this can be resolved... she didn't betray you... you need help... and so does she... no deaths... please... she only tried to help you."

"Help me? She destroyed my soul."

"Giuliana," Luna pleaded, bleeding.

Like a huntress, Giuliana drew back the bowstring. When... out of the flashing darkness, a cry like an animal... a panther say... leapt out... and it was Athena who jumped on her sister from the back and knocked her to the ground. They struggled to the death.

"Reinforcements," Luna said, stricken.

"Yes, my love," I said.

The others were there, encircling us. Dr. Bongo tended to Luna's wound. We carried her into the mansion. Zoo, Brainerd, Hodder, Odd and Arjuna assisted Athena in disarming and subduing Giuliana. The game she was playing was deadly… loveless. She fought like a cat. She was blaming us all for her woes. She was at the centre of her pain… striking out at anybody and anything near her. Her anguish went back decades. But she had it in the most for Dr. S. How she ruined her life and her story. I had already called the authorities… the police knew this place… the neighbours would complain, but I'd deal with their complaints later. I even thought of the Detective and what he would do in such a moment.

Now, for the restraints… Dr. Bongo had been given my key for the medical supplies. He had taken charge of Luna. I injected Giuliana with a tranquilizer. Only Athena cheered. The others looked disturbed. The sky was suddenly quiet, and only a few stars were visible. The fireworks were over. The story emerged of how the group had gotten lost, then with flashes of light from the pyrotechnics, regrouped under Zoo's command and had made it out without finding Giuliana. Athena's hunch was right… Giuliana had never entered the maze. She'd plotted it that way… the plot meant murder. They had helped each other out… they were now tied together in a new tale.

Running through my mind was what there was to deal with. First, there was Luna, next Giuliana, the police investigation, the follow-up and aftermath of the session and the violence, and then the truth. It had always been about truth, as far as I was concerned. Evidence with missing pieces… clues of clues, as the Detective liked to say. The truth was that Professor Brainerd was a secretive man, married to a former student and now colleague, much to the unhappiness of others she flirted with or toyed with or simply was the victim of… that was Professor Hodder with Dr. Bongo Scully by accident when the head incident occurred. The truth was that Odd had been put up to tormenting his professor, Brainerd, thinking it was subversive or artistic, and leading to disaster. His associate, twin, co-conspirator, Arjuna, was the Porter of a different order, arrogant, defiant, thinking he was better than those with position and privilege. He'd never do what he was told… he liked to do the telling… by mirroring… by mocking and imitating… he'd take on your identity to the point of madness… till you came under his control. He opened and closed doors on perception and meaning, only to shut you out. He was the best philosopher… the best lover… the best extortionist… without training or skills. His was an entrenched position. The truth was that Professor Hodder was an academic who would rather be a thug… a lover who wanted to be a fighter… a perpetual loser of arguments… a failed artist… he was never good enough… but liked it that way. The truth was that Dr. Bongo Scully was prodigious… a man of science with more feeling and sentiment than a crybaby. He loved miracles most of all… life was for thinking about, but especially for feeling it… he couldn't hide behind science.

In this case, the truth was they had wounded the healer. In doing so, their stories were shattered to pieces. They must find another way to live. Then another truth presented itself: this case had made me fall in love with the wounded healer. The pyrotechnics were over—the crew wanted to be paid. An Italian, Massimo, was now standing in front of me, smiling.

"Did you like the light show?"

"Splendid," I let him know as he wished to know.

"And?"

"And?"

"And will you engage us again, Dr. Wango, for let's say, a wedding?"

"Oh, yes, for a wedding, or for a party at the end of the world… whichever comes first… certainly fireworks. Here is your fee and a little something else for the trouble. But please hurry… so you will not be swept up in the investigation."

He took the envelope I handed to him, and with the word "investigation" was gone. I looked in on Luna. Wounded, but alive. I loved her. I wanted nothing but for her to love me. That would take time… like healing her wound.

The police were here. They knew their job. They apprehended… they questioned… they wrote up the events… the witnesses… the testimony… read the rights… and moved on with their work. They had the weapon. They had the perpetrator. They had the victim. They wanted her in a hospital under guard. Dr. Bongo made the call and Luna was taken by EMS to Dr. Bongo's hospital. She asked to be taken to the Wellness Centre, and I told her she would go once she'd been treated and discharged.

"Will you come with me into the woods?" she asked.

"I'm already packed," I said and kissed her hand. "My love," I added.

Wound for wound, it was about love. This last Truth Party had come a little too close, and maybe should be the last. I told her so. A farewell to storytelling and mystery was how I put it. She smiled.

No helicopter ride for these folks. They were loaded into a paddy wagon… fun for all… even Zoo. He was a little nervous about whom he might meet at the police station. I assured him she was likely not there.

"Hell," he said.

"Hell, exactly," I said.

Was that the great reveal? Was the great (or not so great) reveal that there was a crisis, falling action, a shootout (or just an arrow shot in an attempted murder), the perpetrator apprehended, those that would condemn us to everlasting hell on earth as unusual suspects questioned? Was it that they stuck to their stories, but that their stories were not their own? Was it that where I set up the action (the nudity, the maze, the fireworks) for the sake of a thriller, a case, ideas barged in on their own, uninvited? Was the great reveal the simple truth that either there was nothing to reveal, or that in life, what was revealed to us in times of suffering was a foretaste of hell? And that, if this revelation was not enough for us, then we must at all costs try love… but love was not a cure (and it was often cited as a cureless disease). Would love keep us safe for a while, as long as it lasted, cradling us in its quick, fresh embrace? Had love made its erotic entrance into our life stories—two doctors in love? I didn't know… but maybe… just maybe, when she healed enough to take me to the Wellness Centre in the woods, I'd find out what Luna knew. Still and all, to love somebody was… *strange* and that bewildering time of my life… the end of my old ways and the beginning of something I couldn't fathom. How would it all end? I didn't know—I mean, I liked a good *cliffhanger*, hanging on for dear life to a surprise ending, and this case's ending was indeterminate. Whimper to bang—we'd had that. Now, it was bang to narrative whimper. How to *best sell* this escaped me for the time being. Though I was not in the business of bestsellers, this story about stories was sold, more or less. It was an easy sequence of *truths,* and not the *Truth.* A Truth Party that revealed there was little or nothing to reveal was perversely my kind of farewell party, celebrating truth as little more (or nothing but)… *Truths*.

3
WILDERNESS VOICES

My sole desire was to know how Luna was and what she knew. I also wanted to know her more intimately. My longing, however, was in abeyance until such time as I'd dealt with the action against other victims, and the case against Giuliana for attempted murder in this and other "group fictions" that had taken place at my mansion. I was implicated, though I'd tried to do some good. But good intentions and the pathways to hell were well documented. In dealing with the police, most of what I knew I must withhold or hold in strict confidence. But I must also let the authorities know what I knew (within acceptable limits) for the sake of the law, truth and justice. The complication was that I was in love with Luna. I wanted to help her so much that it was making me crazy... I was anxious about her wellbeing to such an extent that I was becoming obsessive about her. I wanted her to have the best care. Still, she seemed angry... even spiteful... her view was that she had tried to heal Giuliana and had now become a victim of violence. It was the ingratitude that rankled and riled her the most. Why did she have to bleed for somebody she'd tried to help? Trying to kill the doctor or wounding the would-be healer was a special case and required further investigation. I was not trying to analyze her, but rather connect with her—the involvement of two doctors in love, and that sort of twist, was a little unnerving to say the least. Was it passion? Was it madness? Or both?

Luna wanted to be airlifted to the Mindfulness Wellness Centre North of Lake Superior, once she was treated and released from the hospital for her wound. Dr. Bongo Scully didn't advise the move, but he couldn't prevent it either. I told him I was getting involved... that I was heading there myself... that I hoped to care for her at the facility as soon as possible.

The police were still actively interested in the case... and one of the detectives insisted on looking into the possibility of conspiracy, especially among the group from the university. Odd said he had a "hate on" for academics.

"Only academics with criminal minds," the detective said.

I was curious to see if I could get the criminal remanded to my custody to treat her and try to heal her wounded mind up North. How could I restore her in such a troubled state? How long would she have to stay in custody... with the court case... the whole story coming out... and my involvement in it? Zoo would likely tell me to buy her out somehow, once he'd see how I was implicated, and, instead of being dragged through it, he'd advise me to throw money at the problem to make it go away. What if we failed? How many scenes would she make in her manic way? Her record for getting out of trouble was not good. She liked to complicate and thicken the horror she could create. It was like those cases you read about from the past where "the lunatic" laughs and cries and twitches and jerks and sticks out her tongue and shakes her legs and hates noises and people. You don't want to use the word "hysteria" anymore. You want to talk to her and treat her by talking it out. There are drugs, but what will they do to her in the long run? How harmful is the cure? Will words do the trick? So she'll make faces at you and tell you where to go and how fast to get there. She's likely to use her "masks" and "pouts" and "grimaces"—all of which will drive you crazy for the sake of interpreting what's really going on inside her mind. You know she hates you, has nothing but contempt for you and what you say and do, and what you stand for. You're the enemy and not the one within. What picture will come out about her... about us... from the discoveries made by talking? Her mother? Her father? Their horrid treatment of her? The beauty of her lover? The abuse at the hand of all the bastards she'd ever known? Her malice towards Luna and her bitterness towards Zoo? The weird habits... the way she does or doesn't do sex... the pain that has no relief... the hurt that clings to every fibre of her being. She thinks you don't know her... that because you had fights with her... about her wrongdoings... that you're out to get her... to kill her off... and that you don't care for her. How would any treatment go?

But then again, Giuliana's case was an attempted murder. She was a criminal. To what extent was she responsible for her crime? She had tried to kill her therapist. The means and method were available at my place, the mansion, and the place where I had wanted understanding to happen, the place where I had sought to interpret the human struggles and transform the anguish into the joy of life. I was a lover and interpreter of human attraction. Yet what was the upshot of all that loving and interpreting? Pain.

"I'm culpable for the way things are," I said in a disturbing moment of self-revelation. "I'm to blame... for how things are turning out. I'm filled with remorse. I want everyone safe and sound... in the imaginative struggles for truth... no injuries... certainly no deaths on my watch. But how to prevent pain and loss? And how to forestall the massacre of days and nights in unravelling the human mess? I don't know. Did I ever think I did? What does that poet, Ginsberg, call it in *Howl*? Oh, yes, 'ping pong and amnesia.' Back and forth, we hit the little white ball... over the net... hard and harder to keep it going in the air... and forgetting, just forgetting everything about everything, except the game... why we're playing it and what we hope to happen when we win or lose. I love to interpret the meaning of the game... love it to the point of my personal shame... I can laugh with the mockers and cry with the mocked."

For now, I'd let the law tackle the violent ones and look to help the victim of violence—Luna. I wasn't fit to drive. So I asked Zoo to get me a driver. He obliged and sent one of his standby vehicles—a limo—to pick me up. I asked Ray, the driver, to take me downtown: first, to the hospital, Mt. Sinai on University Avenue, and then the police station. When he dropped me off, I charged in to see Luna. They'd sent her by ambulance to Sunnybrook, the trauma unit, given the nature of her wound. If I'd known, I would have made a beeline for her closer to home. Back in the limo, I asked Ray to head North for Sunnybrook. But when I got there, they wouldn't let me see her just yet. She was also under police guard. I asked Ray to head down to the station for my interview with the police. I'd got an in with my old collaborators—Win and Mij—as I called them. But it was not their case.

I was waiting to be interviewed when I was given the news that Giuliana had, with the aid of her accomplices, made a break for it... she had escaped custody... wild and foolish... and I thought I knew who was likely with her... Odd and Arjuna... a duo known as *Marath*... it was a cell then... conspirators aiming for more than the humiliation of a university professor and the attempted murder of a psychotherapist... Oh, hell... what now? What could Giuliana be thinking of—making matters worse by making a break for it... fleeing... a flight risk... and with that odd duo? The oddity thrilled and frustrated me.

A hunch, a quick guess: they were conspirators practising their own brand (deluded as it was) of radical politics. They'd shoot you or throw a bomb at you as quick as get to know you, believing you were responsible for all the problems in the world… or you were one of the cabal… that deserves to be killed… destroyed. That was the beauty of anarchy—bring it all down. Throw out the baby with the bathwater. Who the hell cared? But what exactly was their involvement with Giuliana? She seemed to shun and snub them both… maybe, for appearance sake… the shooter, the archer that had wounded Luna, her psychotherapist, controlled them… and compelled them to work for her. They were in thrall to her.

I immediately thought of the Detective…. Sir Dragonfly… and wanted him and needed him in on the vexing case. But he was on a kind of honeymoon with Miranda, wasn't he? Well, it was worth a try, given the facts on the ground. Love and duty weighed in him in equal parts. The scales wouldn't tip if I tipped him off to the evidence. So, I made the call.

Revenge had its intimate side, the personal thumps and shocks of recognition and revelation—the reversal of intimacy to the point of betrayal. I mentioned this to the Detective once I had him on the cellphone in connection with my present predicament and personal plight. He said he got it, but was too far away (physically) to attend to my needs for the time being—to meet, to talk things over, to get involved—but said he'd dig into it (beyond looking), and after the excavation, he'd tell me what he'd managed to turn up. It was good to hear him. He was especially interested in the shooting, given his love of archery, and was particularly struck by the suggestion of a conspiracy involving two men claiming to be the same person in relation to the shooter.

"Bye, bye, Detective."

"But only for now," he said.

Ray drove me to Sunnybrook to see my beloved in critical care. I waited and waited… but it was so hard to wait. She was in recovery. Later… much later, I was allowed to visit her. I talked to her. She insisted on telling me things about her past. I told her it was unnecessary. But she was going through something of her own… must have been the drugs… or something she had held inside for years and to get off her chest.

"My mother bought everything in sight," she said, "all kinds of goods… artworks… real estate… people, too. When I was a teenager, she competed with me for my friends… males and females alike. She borrowed cash from everybody in terror of my father finding out. For him, he had his own fears… the way he looked at me… touched me, punished me… and my hidden shame that I liked it… as a way of getting back at my mother. Father used to go berserk threatening to kick us all out… or just kill himself to get it over with. He continued to beat me… as a way of punishing my mother. Pain was desire and desire was pain. I was hospitalized and eventually saw a shrink… came out of it… with zeal to help others… victims of abuse… victims of chaos. Look at me now."

I realised how much I loved her… how attached I was becoming to her. What more would there be to this? If I were her patient, I'd have to pay her for the sessions. Was friendship a form of seduction, especially with the scandal of two doctors in love under these circumstances? It was consuming me—my thoughts couldn't get away from Luna. There was plenty in everything she said and did. Could we really love each other? Or was it only on my side—another delusion? But first, she must heal… she must survive. Thinking of intimacy with the victim of violence—what was going on? What was wrong with me? We didn't really know each other—not enough time to. The destruction of things sometimes leads to this type of crisis. There is a push to destruction in some of us—the self or others. What did I know about her? Was she already with someone else? Could she forget him or her? Did she see anything in me? What did I see in her? She was suddenly my anima. Would she want to return immediately to the Mindfulness Centre, or stay with me? I liked solving problems, but here I was facing problems, though not insoluble, that I found I couldn't solve alone.

As it turned out, and for reasons that still mystify me, Zoo decided to support me as a kind of ally and true partner in taking care of the criminal business and the legal problems at hand. He told me he would take on the case, not necessarily out of feelings for me or anybody, but rather because he wanted it over with as swiftly as possible. He wanted us to get back to real estate. People's mental conditions (and the state of their souls, as he said) were still my concern, and he gladly gave up any right to the matter. I could probe and sound them all I wanted to, so long as he didn't have to. He did, however, blame me for getting him involved in not one but two prosecutions. He went on about indictable offenses, bail hearings, pre-trial procedures, pleas and plea-bargaining and the matter of money, not to mention the aftermath of bloodshed.

So with Zoo working on the criminal prosecution, and the Detective looking into the matter of the fugitive from justice and her accomplices, I could give my undivided attention to my wounded Luna. I'd never seen her in bed before. Her lovely vulnerability as she slept was a spur to my desire. She was a strikingly beautiful woman standing up or lying down. I wanted to know how she was doing. I couldn't imagine that she wouldn't make it, despite the nature of the wound. I couldn't help asking myself why I was involving myself at all? Why not just walk away now? Hadn't I enough problems without falling in love? It was one thing to be in love, and still another for anyone to be in love with you? It was not so much who you think you are as who do others take you for?

"What am I to Luna?" I asked myself.

I didn't know, but I did know that I didn't want her to die. I didn't want to live another minute without her. When she came to, she uttered what sounded like *conspirators, assassins, and destroyers.*

"Why not rest a bit before speaking?" I asked her.

"I want to talk about it," she said, "as a way of getting over it."

So she preferred the "talking cure" to the "love cure."

4
THE WELLNESS CENTRE

A low cloud formation was rolling over Lake Superior. Our jeep was leaving mud-funked tracks and grinding over the long dirt road into the northern wilderness. For the time being, Luna was out of harm. Though weak from the violence and drowsy from the medications, she could write her own prescriptions... so could I... doctors healing themselves. Would she get over it? Giuliana's flight had temporarily taken the act and fact of pressing charges away from her. She insisted she'd recovered sufficiently and was well enough to travel, and that it was best for her to get back home.

"They think you're just relieving yourself, and not really helping them."

"Who?" I asked, but knew.

I knew who *they* were—her patients, and one in particular—Giuliana.

"Ungrateful, vengeful."

"Those you try to help can make you feel awful—betrayed, vague, extinct."

"The hypocrisies behind human attractions and oddities."

"Behind all human events."

"Goes with the territory, I suppose, as you know, Clive."

"Don't I just... like a teacher working with special needs kids getting beaten up most days by the children."

"They can't help it—the kids or the teacher—they go back at it every single day—bruising and being bruised. It's a massacre. I want to get back up north."

North. North has a sort of inevitability about it. Usually, I like staying put—where I am in the south. Travelling north—I'm neither for it nor against it as long as somebody else is doing the travelling or deciding not to leave home.

"As a rule, I don't like taking things as they come," I said to Luna, leaning against the passenger side window.

"You like to live for others," she said, wincing in pain.

"Yes, I do seem to live for others… now I want to live for you… and that implies improvisation, plot twists, contradictions—things as they come."

"Things as they come," she said. "But you don't always like it."

"I don't always like it."

I meant, in part, this ride through the wilderness. But was the wilderness one of those things, as they come, that I didn't especially like? It felt as if we were on the run—not going *to* but getting away *from* something. What else can you do with the mess in your life?

When I told this to Luna she nodded, but wouldn't pick it up for discussion, analysis or even by the way. She was fixed on the road, determined to get to the compound. I didn't know how she was able to drive… arm bandaged in a kind of reinforced sling. She was strong… stronger than anyone else I'd ever known, Hera, excepted. The rough road was forcing Luna to hold on for dear life in the driver's seat, and I was going along, hunched over, jolted, and bracing myself for the ride.

The wilderness compound (the Wellness Centre) looked like a village in the forest. The main building resembled a primitive church. The outbuildings reflected the outer world to the degree that they seemed to be part of the surrounding trees. As soon as we arrived after our harrowing trip, I got a text message from the Detective.

"*Conspiracy*. Be safe."

No use to call or reply… he didn't answer. If it was a warning, and that was how I took his cryptic words, I'd be sure to heed it… but what exactly did he mean? Everywhere: water, trees, sky seemed to threaten me in a conspiracy of wildness. I felt the menace of isolation.

"The water tastes good here," Luna said.

She primed and pumped water from the well—water gushed, surged, plashed. With one hand, she cupped the water, drank, and cooled her face and neck. I was filled with awe, but also with foreboding. She seemed so alone, though we were together. I was thinking about the Detective's curt message. If I'd learned one thing, I'd learned that the Detective was always right. With that view in mind, I said to Luna:

"Be careful."

"Don't tell me what to do," she said, "not on my turf, and not ever."

"You won't do as I say, eh? Or as I do? You don't do what you're told."

"Right."

Right. Right. You can't tell her what to think, or say, or do. She wouldn't do as she was told. Everything she chose to do was right, as far as Luna was concerned, and she was home. She was in charge.

"I don't know the place," I said. "So I sense danger everywhere—water, trees, sky."

"I'll take care of you," she said. "I'll protect you."

I had the Detective's text message informing my caution, my care, my attention, and my bewilderment. His words shaped my actions.

"Where is everybody?" Luna asked.

"Is it unusual that nobody is here to greet you?"

"Very… we have people here… staff and patients… but…"

"Nobody is around to welcome you home, eh?"

Luna was looking hard at the buildings.

"Are there signs of trouble… struggle?"

She didn't answer, but headed into the main building. Nothing… no one. I followed her to the outbuildings. The same… silent, empty, abandoned. Then as we stepped back out, a fierce rush of violent movement blasted against us. Somebody was pinning my arms back—tight—and taping me up. Then two figures leaped on Luna, tackled her to the ground, spread her legs open, and assaulted her. She fought like a wild cat, but was subdued with punches and kicks. They worked hard on her wounded shoulder to force her to comply. Then another figure jumped into our midst. While the two assailants were having their brutal way with Luna, this other aggressor (I knew it was Giuliana, despite the camouflage) was shouting:

"You made me. You invented me. But did your ends sanctify your means?"

"Misbegotten, not made, is how I see it," Luna shrieked in her struggle to free herself from her attackers. "Sanctify? Shit—are you a holy thing? We both know better."

"We do now," Giuliana said. "Unlikely, likely… then legitimize…"

"Justify, is that what you're looking for?"

"I guess."

"Hard to believe, but it's not always about you."

"Come to think of it, it seldom is. It's never about me. I don't belong here, do I?"

"Belong?"

"I don't belong to you."

"Even that…"

"From the first till now, I wanted a sense of belonging, the kind that intimacy allows for, insists on, craves… a sacred vow, tenderness, control in the most beautiful sense… comfort of knowing, arousal and release, relief, relieved of the burden of anguish, even the fear of the fear of death…sex and time, but you're calling it *selfishness*, and that it's not my concern, and doesn't belong to me, and never did, and that it's all just yours. But when you compare me to others, the social beings, the sociable ones, I don't fit in. Amen."

"Giuliana, stop this. Stop them."

"All right, I don't fit. But who am I to you? Answer me. Who am I to you?"

"Somebody that needs healing, desperately. You're a person in pain, attracted to suffering, especially that of others."

"But you never take it away. Only add to it. You're like any tyrant or holy one that offers salvation, but delivers death… killing me… on behalf of all those you have hurt or would hurt in the future… if you were not stopped… I must take your life to keep mine and theirs."

"You've already tried. Isn't that enough."

"Just wounding is failure, and failure is not good enough."

I was struggling on the ground. They had bloodied me in subduing me. My fate was duct tape.

"Stop," Luna said when she could.

Would they kill her? Was sexual assault the means to sanctify Giuliana's hate?

"Now, you feel me," she shouted. "Now you feel me."

It was rape. What did she want poor Luna to feel?

"I feel you. Stop them. Stop this, you monster."

"You're the monster."

In a moment of violence, you realize the perpetrator is not scared— you are. You are scared to death. But then it comes to you in a flash that, despite the fear (or because of it), someone else needs you more than you need life itself. They are assaulting Luna; her cries, her imprecations, her fight are not helping her, but aiding them to humiliate her and to dish it out, to lay her low, kill her, if they have it… destroy her.

"Finish her off," Giuliana wailed. "Then him… and burn this place to the ground and all the wilderness surrounding this monstrosity."

Strange was the sound of her ordering destruction. But you couldn't afford to be strange yourself. You must not give in to incoherence during the fight of your life and the life of your loved one. The attraction was more powerful than ever. I had been in this situation before— bound and gagged, taped up, like a human package. I knew I couldn't escape by my own efforts alone. My lips were sealed, my mouth, too; body, constricted, confined. The will to survive, to escape, to set things right surges within you, wanting to explode, even as you are forced to remember, forced to relive the past, the disappointed paradise of what was lost, all the frustrated effects of all the vicious causes where there is nothing to be found. The Detective came into my mind, and then when I thought I had no one to turn to, I heard the whirring of a helicopter above me. Shouts. Whizzing of arrows. Lamentation of people struck. Wounded animals, going down.

The one who cut me loose was the young insect-like man we used to call Dragonfly. He had prevailed.

"Luna, Luna," I said, breathing hard.

"There," he said. "Look to her."

The Detective had wounded Giuliana. The rapists had fled.

"I pierced one of them, too," he said. "The chopper will track them… apprehend them. I have been striving to arrive for days."

"Here you are," I said.

"Here I am."

He bound Giuliana's wrists together with twist ties. He dressed her wounds. I took care of Luna, battered, beaten, violated.

"Her people will be here soon," the Detective said. "They were held not far from here in the boathouse. They suffered abuse, but they'll be able to help."

"Why was she so violent?" Luna demanded. "Why was she violent?"

I was trying to comfort her, to deal with her wounds. She couldn't move her bandaged arm. She was almost completely naked. Then the Detective's companion, Miranda, rushed towards us.

"We need a rape kit," she said. "Get her to a hospital."

"We're better than this… we're better than this," Luna, in distress, was chanting.

I knew she wanted to understand it: the violence and savagery. She had worked with her attackers. Why hadn't she seen this coming? She couldn't blame herself. She shouldn't. But she did. Abuse? Abuse. She had been wronged.

For unknown reasons, something haunted me in the form of words,

words I'd read in the past: "God is the pain of the fear of death." They were no longer afraid to die, and so had played God. And in doing so, had made matters worse. How could a doctor like Luna be implicated in the making of such creatures? What was my part in it? As for me, I had tried to do some good, but the results were disastrous, horrifying, and terribly and dreadfully wrong. I began to cry, uncontrollably, inconsolably. I was crying in the wilderness.

The Detective had managed to free Luna's people from their shackles and humiliating confinement. They were in varying degrees of pain and anguish. Many of them were in bad shape. They were healers, not fighters. But they rallied to assist Luna, Dr. S. Their beloved Dr. S. was taken to the main building for treatment. They had to deal directly with her trauma. They tried to stabilize her until medical staff was able to measure the extent of the damage done and take care of her. She was doubly wounded… in body and mind.

The Detective had also coordinated the police search for Odd and Arjuna, the co-conspirators, the rapists. I felt dreadful, implicated. My intervention had gone wrong. But still and all, what had gone wrong with these young men with their conspiracy theories and thrill-kills? Why all the violence and bloodshed, not only here in the wilds, but in the cities around the world? What had happened to unleash the Saturday Night Specials and assault rifles, the arsenal of chaos and massacre? Not to mention the Sunday night suicides in market places, nightclubs and restaurants? But the helicopter search made its first strike. Odd was unable to escape. Perhaps, he had surrendered before dying. Arjuna had not. Apparently, he had died from a self-inflicted wound. A hunting knife had ended his flight.

5
RENUNCIATION

"In the stone there's no pain, but in the fear of the stone there is pain. God is the pain of the fear of death. Whoever conquers pain and fear will himself become God."
—From *The Possessed* by Fyodor Dostoyevsky (translated by Constance Garnett)

Disaster. It was a massacre. Not what I wanted... had wanted... not at all what I had hoped for, and intended to happen. My aim had been peace and reconciliation. The intention was the curative power of storytelling. It had not cured these people. It was too literary to provide the help they needed. Luna needed to be cured in a way that fiction could not provide for. I couldn't keep from thinking that my life was a carnival of suffering animals... and that I was the ringmaster of the carnival of human oddities.

Carnival of human oddities? Was sickness a carnival? Was human suffering a show, a spectator sport? I'd never sought to make trouble. Was I meant to be an agitator? Was I working for the wrong side? Was I not a peaceful man, a peacemaker? Why wasn't I an agent of good? Nothing could soothe my irritation but that. I was sore. I'd tried to be kind, thoughtful, and enterprising; but my energy was spent, and my efforts had come to *this*. I was disappointed by violence—the waste of goodness in the criminal hearts of those who cannot help. But in the multifarious routes of life and the vagaries of my existence and my vain attempts to help and heal others, I suppose I had made trouble for others and myself. I was the hell I had tried to keep us from. I'd tried to smooth things over, but in reality, I had created bumps and set landmines (consciously or unconsciously) for their destruction—the result appeared to be the same.

Why had I offered myself as a stand-in for Zoo only to be taped up, roughed up, kicked around... needing to be rescued? I hadn't solved the case. The Detective had. Why had I offered sanctuary to a pack of intellectuals, hell-bent on revenge? Why had I fallen in love at my age with someone who didn't want me? Why had I caused the suffering of so many? Giuliana's illness—why unleash it? Arjuna and Odd's repression—why trigger its dangerous darker forces?

"I've been the catalyst," I said to no one in particular. "I'm responsible for the pain… and though intent on relieving suffering I've caused it and helped to deepen it. No solace. No consolation. No cure. I've made a carnival of sickness. I've made things worse… worse than worse. The worst has come to the worst under my direction. I'm the prime mover of pain. What is it that I used to say: it is an easy sequence of truths, but not the Truth. A Truth Party—what gave me the right? A party that reveals there is little or nothing to reveal is my kind of party—truth as nothing but dead truths. I've lived long enough to know that the lover and interpreter of stories failed at what he wanted most to do—yes, the storyteller is a deceiver, but the interpreter and lover is worse. He's a fraud. To repudiate the tale and the teller becomes part of the new story, darkness becomes darker still to the point of revulsion… it is inescapable… the lover gets love wrong, not right… and the interpreter does not get the interpretation right, but wrong… therein lies the sadness and the horror. And what of the fear of the pain of death? I've killed with it, wittingly or unwittingly. I'm at fault. I have wronged these people. I've hurt you. I haven't righted the wrongs—I've added to the losses. I've used my resources—my money, my time, my so-called philanthropy, and my success… to devastate others. No grace. No forgiveness. No reconciliation. Simply wrong. I must have believed that I was always right, and yet I was not… I was and am wrong."

I must surrender to the authorities—or get the Detective to put me out of my misery… an arrow through the heart… no, the mouth… I was too cowardly to end my own miserable life… playing the lover and interpreter… playing God… playing peacemaker… playing doctor. I'd give anything to get out of this, but the massacre was evidence against me. All clues led to me… as always. What was my crime? I cared… I care… but I was wrong… I am wrong. Now, as a result, Luna will not see me. I declared my love for her, but she turned me away… ordered me to get out… never to see her again. Never. She gave me up. She has given me up.

What about Luna? Arrangements have been made for a D and C. For the sexually criminal action taken by her assailants against her, the only one to survive is Giuliana. She will pay the price. But I was as guilty as she was by implication. I couldn't stop it. The thing of it was: I still wanted stories to cure us. But can they? If so, what is the illness… the disease? Life? Love? What? Lack of empathy? No imagination? Is it a new way of thinking about the same old things? Is it the truth of infatuation with a storyteller? Is it a love affair with the characters, the plot, and the curative power itself… as in music, art, or just walking for an hour each day?

But there was blood on my hands. I couldn't wash it off. I was implicated in the horror of what had happened. I was responsible, and the force and weight of that responsibility were bearing down on me, crushing me. It was no surprise then when the Detective advised me that I was under suspicion. He said that he would speak for me, but that it was best not to say anything to incriminate myself until I had a chance to call in a good lawyer. Was I innocent? It was a culpable innocence, at best, but it was guilt, shame… responsibility. Was I a flight risk? Should I try to get away, throw money at the problem until I could extricate myself from the tangle, the coil and snare that I had put myself into?

"I'm a mischief-maker," I found myself shouting at the top of my lungs to the wilderness that surrounded me. "I'm a dealer in lives… in stories. It amuses me to play with others and the stories of their wretched lives. It pleases me to be thanked. Thank you, Dr. Wango… thank you for nothing. Is that a good insanity defense? Is this a renunciation? I'm addicted to the pain of others… a fake Christ… a complex without faith… has my considerable wealth comforted me? I can look down on others from a great height. I can buy things and people—order them to do as I wish, which I claim is for their own good, but which I know is really for my own good. What good is that? No earthly good at all, Dr. Wango. It has made me feel superior, though, in fact, I'm inferior. I go begging at my own door. What for? To have it slammed in my face… my hand bitten even as I offer it in a gesture of giving or in friendship and greeting."

I never for a moment suspected that it would be like this—that it was supposed to turn out this way. I never wanted to deceive or cheat anybody. But I cheated the cheaters and deceived the deceivers.

"It's a fetish," I said, hurling abuse at myself and at the empty sky. "I kiss their feet… or their asses, as some would have it… I stay kneeling long after I've kissed their extremities. Down on my knees is where I belong. Now spurned in love… rejected by Luna… with dead bodies in a place of wellness and healing… losses everywhere… everything in ruins. I have nothing but shame for myself… covered in it…. and contempt. How can I stop being myself? It took so long to accept who I was and am… and now I must turn my body inside out. I must confess… no one else is to blame… they are sick… not cured… not responsible… I am… but I am not qualified to heal them… to declare them sane… healthy… Are the dead sane or insane? I've made a mess of it. Arrest me. Try me. Lock me away. Set them free. There wouldn't have been rape, murder, suicide, if I hadn't begun 'healing' them. They are not rapists. I am. They are not killers. I am. They are not suicides but my victims. I can't kill myself. The suffering would be over. I want it to last… to go on and on… for my sake. I am guilty. It all started when nobody could say 'No' to me, and then I couldn't say 'No' to anyone. Yes, 'yes' is to blame. I kneel at the feet of affirmation—the fear of saying 'No' to the world… of agreement, approval, and concession. I do what you want, secretly resentful of my decision to get it for you… to do your bidding. What is it but the bidding of the insane? Human oddities… and I serve your special interests. I'm your provider, pimp, and enabler. By serving you, I have become strange, weird, and odd. I am in a carnival of human madness. Mad North-by-Northwest… the lost paradise. Snub me. Shun me. Do what you want to me. I give you my permission. Let it be a public humiliation, a public execution. Behead me, like that pathetic professor that carries his big head against the absurdity of life. I won't carry my head. I won't pick it up and walk. But stay down in the dirt as I was meant to. Kick my head into the mud… the shit."

That was when I began shouting these thoughts aloud to the point of raving. I was spewing my venom. All the hurt… all the bile… all the hate and self-loathing at my complete inability to do what was right. It was the moment that the Detective had been waiting for. He called my name several times, as if to wake me from my nightmare. Then failing that, he lunged at me. I struggled with him… fighting for no reason than to hurt myself. Let him suffocate me…

"Kill me," I said. "Don't make a mistake and let me live. I'm guilty… I'm what is wrong with this world. Not the tyrants…. They can be shot or hanged, but the false healer… the destroyer of goodness…. Good intentions that mask failure. Do me a favour. Get rid of me. My decadence was my comfort… my lording it over others… my science…

my control... my generosity, which was a front for my need... my greed to destroy you... kill you... or help you to kill yourself... with kindness. I've wanted too much. Still do. I've eaten too much. Drunk too much. Pleasured myself to excess. I've taken too much and given away too much."

It was then I blacked out, or was subdued, rendered inert, incapacitated, and shown to be the useless thing I really was. Only blackness was useful for the mind in torment. Forgetfulness. Oblivion. A nanosecond, a minute, hour, day, week, month... I didn't know how long I was out cold. When I came to, someone said:

"I'm going to put a tube down your throat to let the blood..."

I passed out... and in this state, which was a dream within a dream, which was a nightmare, which was a chain of nightmares, linked to the hidden reality of my complete shock... collapse... falling, falling into an abyss of my self and the self within myself, trapped in a mineshaft of collapsing ground and putrefaction. In the bottomless pit were dark, deadly voices and hellish faces tormenting me: out popped Zoo accusing me of turning tail and running away from reality into unconsciousness... running away from a mess that I had made... and hiding in my despair... and the Detective endlessly questioning me about what I knew and did not know about Giuliana, Luna, Odd, Arjuna, and the others, the conspiracy of storytellers that lie to us about everything... and the police voices pepper-spraying me with accusations... how these things occurred at my mansion and at the Wellness Centre... under my watch... and more conspiracy theories about my involvement ... and Luna's voice telling me to get lost... and that she gave me up... once and for all... and my own ruined voice accusing and condemning myself.

Was this sleep in the aftermath of trauma? Was it the mind returning to itself to protect me from utter collapse... madness creating a shockproof cocoon... embedding me in blind unconsciousness? When would I see again? When would I wake up? I had abandoned my own story—traitor, conniver, and intriguer. I was a fraud. My conscience was impure. I had broken my promises. I had lied. I failed. I had failed everybody. Madness penetrated my seemingly invincible self-possession... my knowledge... my actions... in a tomb... the prison walls of my pain.

6

A PLACE WHERE IT RAINS INSIDE

W eeks of recovery at the Wellness Centre… weeks of lawyers' talk and court proceedings. Lawyered up, Zoo was the ringmaster in that realm… that carnival of justice and injustice… nothing, more or less, than a freak show—a carnivalesque showdown between sanity and insanity, truth and illusion. With each turn of the screw, each twist in the tail/tale, the pain intensified. The doctor was sick. Days and nights in my own solitary confinement became an outcry of suffering. But what about the criminal rampage? Giuliana was not gone, but incarcerated. She would plead not guilty in her insanity defense. Arjuna was gone, and Odd, gone. I was responsible. My conscience was not clear. It seemed false. What was the truth? I needed to see it, desperately. Desperately, I sought an altered state. Once recovered, Luna saw to their burials. Maybe, mine, too, for she had given me up. She had rejected me even before anything had really begun between us. She had asked me to forget her. I remembered to forget Luna. But was it forgetting to remember to do so every day in remembrance of her?

Who should be tried and sentenced to life? I was sentenced to death… well, a kind of living death… alone in my mansion, transported there, isolated, cut off from the world. Then I realized that the story was over… the story had ended. What state was this? Was it a higher plane of consciousness or its destruction? Why were my values in ruins, the ground beneath my feet, moving, shifting, as if in an earthquake? Seismic collapse, as it were, of tectonic plates, but only within. Layers collapsing… I was on my guard against myself… against a new story. Danger was everywhere. On my degradation, it was like saying, begging: "Forgive me. I forgive you." On my near-destruction, it was a form of pessimism that joined the world's falsely optimistic glee club. They laughed when I cried and cried when I laughed. I was shocked, and in such a state of terror, that I couldn't sleep. What was of value now? What signified anything? What mattered? I didn't know. Over and over, the scenes played in my addled brain. It was endless looping of the past… with nightmares, fear, rage, and helplessness. I was inconsolably sad. Who was I? What was this numbness? Why was I in such danger? What had happened? My fault… my fault entirely… I did not deserve to exist. Let reason and memory go to hell. I was pure reflex. I would call it *paralysis* but for the tears that flowed ceaselessly down my stone face.

Only the Detective's voice pierced my eardrums with the insect sound of solace. Was it a place where it rained inside? Or was that another fantasy? He said he would take care of me until such time… and then Miranda spoke, saying that she would be there to help me and care for me… until such time… as I could care for myself. Until the physician could heal himself, they would stay with me.

But I couldn't say I'd ever been hurt. *Hurt* was a word I couldn't use anymore with impunity and entitlement, especially in connection with myself. The word *grief* was also no longer of any use to me. I realized that when I did something for myself, I did it against someone else. Envy is our greatest creation. Still, would there be a time when one day suddenly I'd say, after the deceit, treachery, violence, abandonment… and even the whisperings of gratitude in the pain of the fear of living, that I'd been wronged? I'd lived long enough to know that the lover and interpreter of stories had failed at what he had wanted to do. In the art of fiction, the storyteller is the deceiver. But the repudiation of the tale and the teller become part of the story. It is inescapable.

"The lover got it wrong, not right," I whispered to the Detective and Miranda. "The interpreter did not get it right, but wrong. I tried to play God."

"Only God is God," Miranda said.

I began to sob, but they told me to lie still… to rest. They told me not to heed my renunciation, but always to believe in the curative power of a new day, a new way with safe passage into tomorrow. The world as I knew it had ended, but the world that I did not know awaited me for its discovery. Yet the cries from my old world still persisted, frightened and haunted me. I was scared and raw to the bone; tired. Yet I'd never been bone idle. I'd always worked hard for others. I had to give up everything and follow a new path. To quote or distort the words of an old poet whose world, too, was gone, I was in need of both the "physician" and the "divine."

"I was wrong," I said. "I was a lover and interpreter of human oddities… now a human oddity myself in my own carnival… nothing but a freak show… and look where it got me… look where I am… and see who I am."

"Only as wrong as we were right," the Detective said. "But now, you're here with us, and in our care. The doctor is sick, and needs a cure. You cried in the wilds, and kept crying. Dry your eyes… no more tears. Your wounded body and tortured mind are more resilient than your current pain. You must see… you must see who you are. We're all implicated in this. We're all responsible. No bystander is completely innocent. In your culpability, you're a man saying goodbye to your life story—or the story you told yourself. It is your farewell to fiction. Disillusionment allows for dissolution… let one worldview dissolve with all its trumperies, but let another new view suddenly appear. Yours was a pseudo-literary interpretation of our lives… the *word* and its relationship to the *world*. This is the end of your enchantment. It is a goodbye to the literature of lies; the book of your own tormented soul, your lie-ography and invented life story. But another *true* story will begin tomorrow."

"Besides, you're a beautiful man," Miranda whispered into my ear. "Who will take care of the Good Samaritan when his time comes to be taken care of? You've always been involved in helping others, at a great personal cost to yourself. This is a quarrel with what you thought or believed you were doing. Yours is a moral passion. It's a debate between the dark motives of your own heart and your sense of responsibility to the world. Let the world and its news spin without you for a while. We'll keep you safe and out of harm. We're not going to let you destroy yourself. The world needs more of *you*. Bye, bye, Illusions. Hello, Truth. Good night, Appearances. Good morning, Reality."

"My friends," I moaned, "I feel forsaken."

"We won't forsake you," Miranda said, touching my hand, as if in blessing. "The liars and the self-deluded need you more than ever. We all need your benevolence."

"You'll get better," the Detective said.

"How do you know?"

"Sometimes you know it's just *Part One*," Miranda whispered, "and not *the End*. You'll get better and better, because you're unique… and you're meant to. We're ministering to a temporarily sidelined ministering angel. Besides, no matter what, it's all for the good."

Here she began singing some kind of Italian song[9] about taking care of me and protecting me. I didn't know whether to laugh or cry at the shy intimacy of her thin, raw voice. But she wanted me to believe her. I tried to do so. The Detective wanted me to close my eyes.

"Now, sleep, Dr. Wango," the Detective said in my other ear. "Sleep."

Sleep, yes, sleep. Was it the cure, as if under a spell in a fairy tale? It was the slumber of self-loathing. I had to wake up from the sleep-induced terror of self-rejection. How ridiculous I must have seemed, crazier than the crazies, in trying to do the impossible. By attempting to do God's work, I had done great harm. I had turned myself inside out. Had I ever done any good? I remembered the Detective once saying with hardly a breath: "It's how it is, and how the world goes."

Zoo knew how the world went. He checked in to see how I was faring. I could hardly look at him, let alone speak to him. It was pride, I suppose, that had led to my self-blinding. When I mentioned it, he said:

"I won't poke fun at an old man's pride. Life will take care of that, or nature or God. We'll all be mocked for our pride."

But he had come to reassure me that all would be well, and that he would do what he could to clean up the mess, and the mess of the mess, his, mine, and everybody else's. He was talking *money*; he told me to hang in there. I was holding on, but just, and still hanging on then. I thanked him by looking directly into his eyes. He left, reassured that, as far as he was concerned, everything would be right again, and he could resume his life, a life in which the mess once made gets cleaned up. When he left, I was filled with the dark sense that those we try to help will beat us. I was beaten by my own need and obligation to be kind.

I managed to send word through the Detective to Luna. I asked him to let her know how grief-stricken I was at what had happened to her, and how implicated I was in her ordeal and suffering. If there was anything I could do to aid in her recovery and in the rebuilding of the Wellness Centre, to please (for the love of mercy) to let me know so that I could do my part. Word came back in a curt message that said: "I'll see." Despite the brevity of her reply, I was thrilled to hear it. Yes, it was about waiting and seeing. It required patience and time in the healing process. We would all *see*. I had always believed that once we could all see and once we had attained precious insight into our life story, we would come to a fitting end. What we do for someone (even

9   "La Cura" by Franco Battiato

for a cause or purpose), we do against someone else or something else.

But I had wanted to love humanity and interpret its absurdity, and here I was vulnerable and at a loss to comprehend what had happened and what was going on. It was as if the whole of my life needed grieving. It was the consciousness of all this that got the better of me and had smashed my moral compass. The Detective was right, he was right, as always, as right as I was wrong. I slept... and after a succession of tomorrows, and further dreams of repudiating my life's work and the story of my life, when I awoke, I picked up my bed, as it were, and walked. I knew what it was to care for another... to look to the comfort of the sick and wounded... and satisfy every need. Now they were taking care of the caregiver. What was operative in my room and in my place was tenderness, as if kindness alone conduced to what was real. Violence and loneliness were the enemies of reality. If I didn't know who I was any longer, they would show me by the action and operation of a tender touch and a kind word my real self. They seemed to sculpt me out of the void. I took shape in darkness... out of despair and loss... formed in the hope of living again... not for nothing, but for the delight of seeing, tasting, smelling, hearing and touching. They touched me. I was touched... and once out of my head, I came back to my senses. I felt like a man carrying my own head in my hands, like a head-carrier of old, like Professor Brainerd that had started it all. I'd been terrified up North in the wilderness so far away from the city. It had borne down on me with its overwhelming weight of violence and solitude. But they had brought me safely back, and, with their gentle spells, had brought me back to life... and to the world. So we could breathe as one... breathe... breathe... as one. As a counterforce to hurt that takes our breath away... we can breathe as one. This was what their tenderness meant... and what it was to be fully human. This was a cure of the plagiarism to the point of despair of life itself and its oppression. I'd never intended that this should ever be about me—not in its beginning and certainly not in its ending. I had wanted it to be about the stories of others, and had to suffer for it now.

"You're not the only one who suffered or suffers," the Detective said.

"No, I'm not," I whispered, "but I never said I was."

"No, but it's your story," Miranda said.

"It's my story," I agreed.

"So stick to it," the Detective added, "and in sticking to it, live, and in living, live on, and in living on, live on and on."

"You can't call back yesterday, or bid time to return," Miranda said. "Accept this moment, and by accepting it, imagine you are happy."

"Imagine it?"

"And *be* happy," she said. "When tomorrow comes, remember that love is all there is, even though sometimes we're forced to sleep with the enemy."

"Welcome to your future," they said.

With the aid of my kind caregivers, the Detective and his beloved Miranda, chanting what sounded like spells from the *Tibetan Book of the Dead* for coming out of darkness into light, I was able to tell the story, free from pain and sadness. The transformative power of their generosity and tenderness fed my mind and freed me from the nightmare. I was not forsaken. I was alive, but not alone. I had to imagine myself happy. Consequently, as the lover and interpreter of human attractions, I was able to write this story down the way I lived it and saw it, truthfully, and so that I could accept the new day and look you directly in the eyes and say in the words of a new story: "I'm telling you the truth."

ACKNOWLEDGEMENTS

I would like to express my gratitude to Louisa Josephine for her help.

Passages and excerpts from other stories were taken from *The Pros & Cons of Dragon Slaying* (Anaphora Literary Press, 2014) and *Dragonfly's Urban Crusade* (Anaphora Literary Press, 2017).

OTHER ANAPHORA LITERARY PRESS TITLES

*The History of British and
American Author-Publishers*
By: Anna Faktorovich

Notes for Further Research
By: Molly Kirschner

*The Encyclopedic Philosophy of
Michel Serres*
By: Keith Moser

The Visit
By: Michael G. Casey

How to Be Happy
By: C. J. Jos

A Dying Breed
By: Scott Duff

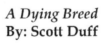

Love in the Cretaceous
By: Howard W. Robertson

The Second of Seven
By: Jeremie Guy

CPSIA information can be obtained
at www.ICGtesting.com
Printed in the USA
LVHW091604300419
616104LV00008B/111/P